ZOMPIRE

VAMPIRE WAR

Bill Rockwell

http://billrockwell.net

Copyright: 2020 William Rockwell
Copyright Cover Art: Thomas Rockwell
Copyright Back Page Insert Art: William Rockwell
ISBN: 979-8645355999

AUTHOR'S NOTE

This story is the second installment in my Zompire series. In the first volume, *Generation Z, Birth of the Zompire,* Master Vampire Quentin DeVoie, bites a human, Damon Drake, in an attempt to convert him to Vampirism. However, the Vampire's Zombies, ignoring DeVoie's orders to bury Damon, try to eat him instead. The combination of the two bites, converts Damon to a Zompire, a combination of these two "Undead Species." Damon, however, retains many of his human characteristics, including a belief in God and a love of humanity. He must then convince his girlfriend, Gabby, and the police, that he represents no danger to her, or to society. Damon enlists their aid in hunting down Vampire DeVoie. Damon and Gabby then destroy both DeVoie and all his zombies.

This volume picks up after the events in *Generation Z, Birth of the Zompire*, and follows the now married couple, Damon and Gabby, as they hunt the remaining Vampires. I have written this segment of their story so it can be read even without reading the first installment. Important events from *Generation Z, Birth of the Zompire* are summarized so the reader can understand the story. If you would like to read the full first volume, it is available from my website, or from Amazon.com.

My other novels include Mysteries, Fantasy YA novels, a Fantasy Religious Novel, and Children's Picture Books, involving Puppies. Visit my web site (http://billrockwell.net) to read the summary and first chapter of any of these. Enjoy *Zompire, Vampire Wars*, and please review it. Thank you.

DEDICATION

For Jonathan Frid, Vampire Extraordinaire,
Star of the T.V. show
"Dark Shadows."

Psalm 3

How many are my foes, O Lord
How many are rising against me!

ZOMPIRE: The combination of a vampire and a zombie, caused by the person being bitten by both of these undead fiends…or being bitten by a Zompire only!

CHAPTER 1

THE BROWN WOLF

The large, brown wolf with reddish highlights charged through the woods, its fur swaying back and forth with each of her movements. Her large, blue eyes searched the path ahead for any sign of danger, or an easy prey to satisfy her growling stomach. She sniffed but sensed nothing. *Most prey animals sense me before I can get within reach, and hide, as they are now. It doesn't matter! I'm in a rush to get home, anyway.*

She hurtled over a fallen tree, and then, in one huge bound, cleared a flowing stream. Spotting her home, a ranch style house, covered in yellow siding with light blue shutters, she slowed to a crawl. Head raised, she sniffed the air. Again she sensed nothing. She sniffed again. There it was! Her husband's scent wafted from the direction of their home. Her huge tail swayed more quickly back and forth with the scent she enjoyed the most. She had tried to smile as the wolf and other animals, but failed. At least the tail wagging gave her some satisfaction that she remained human beneath this façade of Zompire-wolf. Like natural wolves, she couldn't raise her tail above her body, but she could at least show pleasure in its movement.

In two more bounds, she found herself standing before the front door. She shook her head like a dog shedding water from a bath. Slowly, she turned to the rear to ensure that no one had followed her. She sniffed the air once more to be sure. If someone had followed her, human, or animal, she would have turned upon them in an instant to destroy them. Not that their home was a secret. On the contrary, they had tried their best to become part of the community, and even invited people to their home for a visit. People refused, still thinking of the Zompires as vampires. The Zompires were ostracized and avoided. She shook her head again to get the negative thoughts out. She didn't succeed.

She then morphed into the lithe woman she had been before become becoming a Zompire. Her

6

husband, Damon, had granted her this Zompire morphing ability when, at her request, she had begged him to inject some of his already converted Zompire blood into the veins in her long, slim neck. Damon had been converted to a Zompire when the evil vampire, Count DeVoie, had bitten him, and DeVoie's zombie slaves had bitten Damon before he had converted to a vampire. Gabby thought of their hunt for DeVoie. She smiled at the irony of that situation. She and Damon were in the process of destroying the fiends when a zombie had bitten Gabby. At the edge of death, she had begged Damon to bite her, knowing this would convert her to his Zompire wife. In her mind, it had been far better to become a hybrid creature with characteristics of both vampires and zombies, than a mindless, flesh and brain-craving zombie-monster, or a blood-sucking vampire. Now, she smiled. *I was right then, and have never regretted my request since.*

Gabby now wore dark slacks with a black belt and a loosely fitting yellow blouse. Black flat shoes completed her outfit. She often wondered where her clothes went whenever she morphed into a bat, wolf, or any other animal. She ran her fingers through her long, curly red hair, and entered their home through the unlocked door. Her husband's aroma again filled her nostrils. *Have to love that man. I always have!* She stopped after a few steps. *What is that odor? Not Damon. It's vaguely familiar but I can't put my finger on it.* She shrugged. "Damon, I'm home. Can I see you a minute. We've got something important to discuss."

Damon looked up from the stove. He wore worn jeans and a red flannel shirt above white sneakers. Becoming a Zompire had changed his black hair to a light brown that now matched his deep-set eyes. His massive biceps flexed beneath his rolled shirtsleeves. He lifted the cast iron skillet from the stove, and turned toward Gabby's voice. *Funny, I didn't sense, or smell, Gabby's arrival. I usually can. Must be the strong food odor overwhelming Gabby's scent.* "Sure, I'm in the kitchen, working on dinner. You want me to come to you, or do you want to watch your dinner cook?"

Her eyes sprang open. "Cook? Yuck! I'll pass on dinner if that's the case. You know I only like raw food now…hint, hint."

Damon appeared at the doorway to the kitchen, wiping his hands on a dishtowel. "Oh, I know your tastes as well as my own. We both crave raw, dripping, tasty, blood red meat."

CHAPTER 2

RAW BRAINS

Gabby stood with her hands on her hips like a mother disappointed with a misbehaving child. "And so, why are you *cooking* my dinner, instead of going out, and catching some wild animal, so we can feed? For that matter, why not go to the grocery store, and buy some raw meat, say a juicy steak, and throw that down onto my plate, as we've done every night since our marriage? You know what I really feel like right now? That would be some...brains...yes, raw brains." She scrunched up her face. "I want brains...like something that might be desired by...the zombies that attacked me. Oh, my God, I want brains too. Am I turning into a zombie?"

Damon smiled, and gently grabbed her shoulders. "Well, Mrs. Gabrielle Drake, that's exactly what I'm preparing for you, both steak and raw brains. We're going to try cow brains to see if that satisfies us. I want them too." He shrugged. "If not, I'm not sure what we're going to do. We'll cross that bridge when we come to it. Hope you're hungry. We can always survive on the raw steaks we've been eating, but I thought that if cow brains tasted good, then we'd be ahead of the game. As Zompires, we're partial zombies. So, it only makes sense."

"So, what *were* you *cooking*?"

"Vegetables. I used to love cooked spinach and carrots." He shrugged. "It's worth a try."

She gave him a small peck on his cheek. She loved to smell him whenever he applied his after-shave lotion. Getting this close became unnecessary after she developed a heightened smell from her Zompire conversion. She could smell him from miles away, but she still enjoyed being this close. She hoped she always would. "Talking about it has made me so ravenous, I could take a bite out of you, blood, muscle, and even your brains." She squinted at him. "You do have them, don't you? You look very delicious to me right now."

"Save that meal for our bedroom later. Right now, dinner is ready." He pulled her closer, kissing her full lips, tasting the woman he loved, arousing himself. He pushed her to arm's length, and closed his eyes. "Whoa! Down, Boy."

Gabby smiled. "That's supposed to be my line. Isn't it?"

Damon opened his eyes. Before him stood a picture of love itself. He ran his fingers through her hair. "I'm so lucky to have you. I don't deserve you."

"You're right. You don't, and I don't know why I stay with you, but there must be a reason. Maybe it's

10

because you're so handsome. Maybe it's because you're a good provider. Oh, wait. I'm as good a provider as you, maybe better."

"Now, Love, let's not go there right now. You're making this marriage sound one sided."

She punched him lightly in the chest. She felt his large chest muscles. "You know I'm kidding, but since we're the only Zompire couple we know of, it's better we stay together in any case."

"Is that the *only* reason you stay with me?"

"Nope! I love you, and always have. Since my love grows deeper each day, I will kill you, and devour your flesh if you ever attempt to leave me."

He shook his head behind hands held in a stopping motion before his face. "*That* would never cross my mind."

"Better not."

"Oh, I hear you, Oh Great Love Of Mine!"

She tapped him on his chest again. "I have something very important to discuss over breakfast, but first, I'm famished. Let's eat whatever you've prepared in that kitchen of yours before I eat what little brains you have."

CHAPTER 3

ZOMPIRE "SUPERHEROES"

As they ate their raw steak, brains and vegetables, Gabby smiled. "Okay, so, you *do* know how to satisfy a girl's hunger. Where did you get the cow brains, from the farmer down the road?"

"No, of course not! If I killed one of his cows, and took its brain, he would call the police, and they would think of us, and pay us an unwanted visit. I went to the grocery store in town. They have a nice selection of brains."

"I would never have thought of that." She took a large bite of the steak. "The reason I'm home early is I ran into Detective Nolan, Father Coulter, and, believe it, or not, nurse Marge outside the Post Office. They were all there mailing something. I don't know what." She shook her head. "It doesn't matter." She took another bite of the delicious, raw brain, savoring it in her mouth before biting, and swallowing it. "Anyway, Nolan asked how we were coming with our vampire quest." She shrugged. "I told him you were getting a lead on where they had located their headquarters, and that, as soon as we knew, we'd let him know. I hope all that's true. You did say your informant was getting back to you this morning. Right?"

"Yup. He called a little while ago. I think he's afraid to come over, afraid I'm going to bite him, or maybe eat his brains. Who knows? Anyway, they're in a town about 60 miles from here in the hills of Connecticut somewhere. They've cut a large cavern into the mountain, and are holed up there. They've been grazing on local victims occasionally, preferring to catch their prey farther away. I guess they feed their zombies from the brains from far neighboring communities also to avoid being detected by the local authorities."

"So, that's why we haven't heard of many attacks."

"Correct. They can't live like us, eating raw meat and animal brains. It has to be the real thing, human all the way. They've been very careful choosing their victims. My informant said they have the local police and Medical Examiner in their pockets, paying them ing gold, if you can believe it."

"Gold! Wow! Where are they're getting that?"

Damon raised his eyebrows. "I have no idea. They're apparently using it to bribe lawyers to keep them out of jail. I guess we'll have to ask them where their supply is before we destroy them."

"Spoken like a true Zompire, Damon, The Vampire Slayer, My Hero, but let's not bother with the questioning. Let's destroy them first." She sighed loudly, then smiled, and shoved a piece of blood-soaked steak into her mouth, her fangs growing longer with each morsel.

"*Vampire Slayer*? I wouldn't go that far. Maybe *vampire hunter* would be a better moniker.

"You can call yourself, and both of us for that matters, anything you want, as long as we're on the winning side."

He shook his head as he put the last piece from his plate into his mouth. "I can't see how we can lose. No matter how many there are of them, we have the element of surprise, and can hunt them in the daylight." He sighed. "If we're lucky enough to find them during those daylight hours, we can destroy all of them without even a fight."

"And the zombies? They're not destroyed by sunlight."

He leaned across the table, stabbed the last piece of steak from her plate, and presented it to her lips. "Since the best way to destroy them is to shoot them in the head, I think we should both carry guns. I understand beheading them, or burning them, also works, but I think if there are a lot of them, we're better off with guns." He leaned back in his chair after she took the morsel. "For that matter, beheading and burning would also work for the vampires, if we can get them to stand still long enough to behead, or set them on fire. For the zombies, a bullet to the head should work fine."

She shook her head. Her long hair struck her cheeks several times. "Guns? I'm not that great a shot. Remember the zombie I shot happened to be on top of me at the time. It's hard to miss at that distance, but from afar? No way!"

"That means we'll have to get close enough to do the job. After all, they can't hurt us by biting us. We crossed that bridge a long time ago." He smiled, and shook his head slowly. "Neither a vampire bite, nor a zombie bite now affects either of us. That makes us *Superhero Zompires*."

Her eyes sprang open. "Superheroes? You must be kidding! A superhero is someone who saves someone's life, or saves the world somehow."

"So, we'll save all humanity, the whole planet, from this vampire and zombie plague. Yes, we're superheroes, or soon will be."

"Don't let it go to your head though. There's a lot about this Zompire thing we don't know. For all we know, one day we may both turn into zombies, and have our limbs and faces fall off. Yuck!"

He frowned for almost a full minute before speaking. "I hope not, but we shouldn't worry about that now. There's nothing we can do to prevent it, or even guess what's going to happen. So, I say, full speed ahead, and let's destroy some vampires and zombies."

She saluted. "Yes, Captain Damon, but let's try to destroy *all* of the vampires and zombies on this trip so we can get on with our lives, but no guns! I know I would shoot myself in the head, or maybe shoot you. God forbid! Maybe we should bring some of our police friends along for the bullets-in-the-head-idea."

Damon nodded. "I guess it's fortuitous, then, that you ran into our detective friends."

"Father Coulter asked for you since he hasn't seen you in Church lately."

"I've been too busy to go."

She shrugged. "That's no excuse, and you know it. Both Father and Marge wanted to accompany us on our vampire hunt." Gabby paused, and looked Heavenward. "Although they were a great help last time against both Vampire DeVoie and his zombies, I thought it would be a bad idea. I told them they should stay here. It would be safer."

Damon smiled. "Knowing the good Father and Marge, I'm sure they'll find a way to come along no matter what we say."

"My thought exactly. Their presence will undoubtedly make our job harder since we'll have to protect them while fighting our adversaries."

He shrugged. "Can't be helped though. We'll just have to cope."

Loud groans from outside their front door attracted both Zompires' attention.

CHAPTER 4

ZOMBIE ATTACK

Several loud knocks followed the groans that had interrupted breakfast.

Gabby stood. "I'll get it. Must be the neighbor next door. Maybe he has some brains for us to eat."

"Don't get your hopes up. I told you he tries to avoid contact with us. It's more likely a delivery from FedEx, or UPS."

The moans continued, louder than before.

"We'll see."

Gabby yanked the door open. Her eyes popped, and her jaw dropped. Before her, stood a bent over, drooling zombie. Its face melted from its skull like candlewax from the heat of a nearby fire. It struggled to stand upright. The zombie stared at Gabby, its gaze focused behind her, as if studying Damon. Its muffled and gravelly voice echoed from deep within its throat. Gabby found it difficult to understand even though she had superior Zompire hearing. She turned one ear toward the zombie.

"Message from Grand Master Fabian." Its lips barely moved. "He *demands* both of you come to his headquarters to discuss…the future…your future with him."

Gabby growled. "We don't take orders from any vampire, your *Grand Master Fabian* included."

The zombie shook his head very slowly, as it tried to remember something. "Master said you might say something like that. Told me to deliver this message in that case." He reached behind his back, and produced a machete. He thrust it into Gabby's stomach before she could move. The steel blade rocketed through her body, its tip emerging from her back coated with red blood.

Gabby moaned, as she tried to bend at the waist, but stopped because of the increase in pain the motion caused. She stepped back, and fell to her left onto the floor, continuing to moan.

Damon rushed to her side, bending on one knee beside his love. The zombie walked into the house, followed by ten more.

Their grotesque groans filled the entire home. "Brains! Kill Zompires. Master orders them killed. Eat Zompire brains. Bring back Damon's blood on machete. Ugh."

Damon stood, and grabbed the first zombie by the throat. He punched the zombie in its temple. The top of the zombie's head exploded across he room, painting the other zombies with its blood and brains. Those hit by the brains slowed long enough to lick the detritus from their faces. They then continued their relentless, asymmetric, zombie march toward Damon. Their unfocused stare never changed.

Gabby's eyes deepened in their orbits. They became bright crimson. The shine gave a red tint to the floor around her. Ever darkening circles propagated around her eyes. Her brow, wrinkled by her painful expression, smoothed out as the dark circles spread up toward her flaming red hair. The color washed out to a white, paler even that the skin of the attacking zombies. The rest of her exposed skin became whiter than snow. She reached for the machete's handle, took a deep breath, and yanked it from her abdomen. She arched her neck, a high-pitched groan emerging from her as she did so. She didn't bleed further from the resultant hole in either her front or back. Instead, the wounds healed spontaneously, fastening closed like a zipper almost as fast as they had been formed.

She rolled onto her right side, and forced herself to a kneeling position. Black drool fell from her mouth as she stared at the floor. Her head snapped up. She snarled at her attackers. She jumped to her feet, and turned to face the zombies, now growling like wounded animals as they trudged toward Damon. She grabbed Damon's shoulder, yanking him back.

"Let me at the bastards!"

CHAPTER 5

ZOMBIE-DESTROYING ZOMPIRE

Damon turned in an instant when the hand touched him, ready to strike whoever had grabbed him. Recognizing Gabby, he attempted to turn back to their attackers.

Gabby, however, pulled him back. She stormed past him, striking the zombies with her fists, and kicking those not within her reach. She smashed any zombie heads she could reach between her palms. These shattered as if they were eggshells. Their almost pure black, walnut sized brains squished, the grey-black contents shooting onto her and Damon alike. She crushed a few heads against the wall. Their brains smeared toward the floor. She picked up the machete, and chopped the tops of the remaining zombies' heads off, one at a time, as if they were ripe pineapples.

The entire confrontation lasted only a few minutes. When all the groans were silenced, she stood among the broken zombie bodies, spinning in place to ensure all had been crushed by her fury. Satisfied she had destroyed their enemy, she took a deep breath, looked upward, and sighed. She dropped the machete.

Over the next minute, her normal skin color returned, red eyes morphed to blue, her eyes ascended from their deepened sockets to their normal position, and the blackness surrounding them faded to her normal, light skin color. Her hair morphed from white to red, migrating from her forehead to the end of every hair. Her breathing started again. She placed a hand on her chest. "I didn't even notice I was holding my breath."

Damon placed an arm around her.

She again surveyed her violence. "I guess we won."

"*You* won, Gabby. They never stood a chance against…whatever you became…the angry, zombie form of a Zompire, I guess."

Gabby's jaw fell open. "Zombie?" She shrugged. "Maybe."

"No maybes about it. Remind me never to get you angry at me."

"Never. By the way, did you notice how small those zombie brains were? You suggested shooting them in the head. You'd have to be very, very lucky to hit that tiny thing by shooting them in the head."

"I'm not sure luck has anything to do with it. Remember our last encounter with a zombie. Shooting it in the head killed it. Maybe the mere fact of fresh air entering the skull cavity is enough to make the brain die. Who knows? Whatever the mechanism, I think it's still a good idea to have our police friends accompany us once we find them to use their guns as weapons against the zombies. Useless against the vampires, of course, but we definitely need all the help we can in this venture." Damon smiled wryly. "Maybe you could turn into your angry-form-of-Zompire. You could destroy an army of zombies." He shook his head. "You looked like you could easily have beaten the crap out of me too."

"It would never cross my mind. By the way, how did vampire Fabian expect us to go to him, since we don't know exactly where his headquarters are?"

"Beats me. Maybe the zombies were supposed to tell us *only* if we agreed to meet. Of course, you said, "No," and destroyed the ones who knew the location."

She smiled. "Remind me to tell that damned vampire that his zombies shouldn't have stabbed me if he *really* wanted us to meet."

"Noted, but maybe, if you said, "No," they were told they should then get my blood on that machete."

"Maybe, but they could have delivered the address before committing Zompire-suicide. So, do you have any idea how are we now supposed to meet him without knowing the location?"

Damon shrugged. "Maybe he's got a backup plan. Maybe we'll get a second visit. Who knows?"

"If there is another messenger, I'm not waiting for the message. I'm attacking first."

"In that case, that messenger is doomed."

She smiled wryly. "If Fabian wants us so bad, he'll have to deliver his address himself. A simple phone call would suffice…and would be safer too."

CHAPTER 6

THE INVITATION

Gabby rested her head on Damon's shoulder. "I could never hurt you like I did them. I don't know what came over me. I got so mad. I couldn't control it. Suddenly, I became more than a superhero…I became a super zombie, unstoppable, unbeatable. Rage spread through my body. I couldn't control it. All I wanted to do was destroy the beasts who had tried to kill me."

"You did that very well." He led her to their soft couch in their living room. "You sit here, and relax a little, if that's at all possible. I'll clean up the mess."

She plopped onto the couch, head resting against its back, her gaze fixed on the ceiling. "Okay. I'll wait here. I'm spent anyway. I need some more of that food you prepared for me. All of a sudden, I'm famished."

Damon made quick work of the zombie bodies, carrying them outside two under each arm. He dumped them into a pile in a clearing far behind their house. When he finished, he doused the bodies with gasoline, and set them ablaze. He stood, watching the blaze until he felt the fire had begun to subside to ensure it didn't

24

spread beyond the initial area. The stink wafted into his nostrils. "Wow! What a stench! Hope my neighbor doesn't catch a whiff."

Returning to Gabby, he found her asleep. He sat next to her for 15 minutes before she awoke.

"Good day, Gabby. Welcome back."

"Back? Back from where?"

"Whatever you were dreaming."

"Didn't dream at all…not after that nightmare." She caressed her healed abdomen, and then pointed to the door.

"Understandable."

She turned her head so she could see him. "I don't understand what just happened. I guess we still don't know what to expect with our new Zompire bodies." She caressed his cheek. "As long as you love me in any form I may take."

"Of *that* you can be assured."

She smiled, pulled his face toward her, and kissed him on his lips for almost a full minute. "Why send zombies, though? The vampires must know we could destroy them with ease…even if I hadn't changed into my angry, zombie-destroying-Zompire."

"I pondered that very question as I burned the bodies. I think they expected us to destroy them, but I don't know why. Telling them to get my blood on the machete was stupid. There's no way they could do that." He paused. "It may have been a message to us that they're after us, gunning for us, so to speak, and there was no real message. They may want us to get mad at them, and come charging after them without a well thought out plan, falling into whatever trap they have waiting for us."

"You're probably right, but it was still stupid, and presumptuous of them to assume they could get us mad." She smiled ruefully. "Well, I guess they did manage to get *me* mad, but you know what I mean."

"Yeah, and I agree…stupid, but also smart. That attack may have been simply an invitation, an invitation to meet with them eventually, winner takes all. In that case, we can expect that second message."

"Okay, given that, what do we do now?"

"Exactly what we had already planned. Give them a visit, walk into their trap, and beat them at their own game."

"Okay, but could we finish our meal first. I'm still hungry. What else have you got for me?"

"I've got anything you want. You need all your strength in case you decide to morph again."

"Amen to that! Let's eat!"

As Damon lifted Gabby from the couch, and headed for the door, the machete on the floor began to vibrate, and ring like a cell phone.

Both Zompires looked at each other.

Without smiling, Gabby nodded toward the machete. "I think it's for you. Answer it. Tell whoever it is that I'm busy eating my dessert." She smiled. "What kind of dessert have you got for me, anyway?"

CHAPTER 7

THE MESSAGE

Without answering her, Damon placed her back onto their couch. He knelt next to the machete. He bent close to it, expecting it to explode. Instead, a red light blinked with each ring. Shrugging, he picked it up, and pressed the red button.

The voice was deep and resonant, sounding like the growl of an angry dog. "Hello, Gabby and Damon, or should I say, Zompires Gabby and Damon? Anyway, I am the Supreme Vampire, Grand Master Fabian Drake, Head of the New England Chapter of Vampires. I ascended to that position, after you destroyed our previous leader, Master Quentin DeVoie, along with his zombie slaves. He came to you in peace. We all desired that you join us, join the forces that will rule this entire planet. I have to assume he told you about it before you snuffed him. You never answered my email, offering you much the same thing. So, you must not be interested in our offer, and, if you're listening to this, you've destroyed our zombie representatives. The machete was my idea, in case you wouldn't listen to our peaceful offer through them. It's a shame you didn't accompany them here.

Maybe you think I'm wrong for not going to you in person, but I thought you might attack first, and not even listen to what I had to say. If you're listening to this, I was right, and you did destroy my zombies. I wish I wasn't right, though. I really wanted you to agree to meet. I had directed them to bring you here, and not attack you, but *only* if you said, 'Yes.' So, please listen to my peaceful offer."

"Peaceful, my ass!" Damon muttered.

"Ditto from this Zompire," Gabby said, standing in the doorway that separated the kitchen from their living room. She nibbled on a frozen piece of blue gray brain that she had found in the freezer. "Go to Hell, Fabian!"

"Pretty sure they can't hear us. It sounds like a recording."

"Turn it off, and join me in this scrumptious frozen morsel. It's better than ice cream."

"Shush. Let me listen."

The recording continued without interruption, confirming Damon's contention that it was a recording. "After your meeting with Master DeVoie, one of the zombies, the one who remained outside as a rear guard for him, made it back to us, and told us of your conversion. Would have never thought that the combination of a vampire and zombie would make a

Zompire, as I understand you're now calling yourselves."

In his mind's eye, Damon pictured the vampire shaking his head, and looking skyward.

"Our current zombie virus, perfected from Master DeVoie's original virus, makes the zombies crave brains and human flesh, and has the added benefit of allowing them to understand and communicate with us on a limited scale…well beyond that achieved by DeVoie's zombies. We also heard that you promised the police that you were going to start a *Vampire War*. I recommend against that. Granted, you defeated one vampire, but we're hundreds, and this is only one branch of us. There are many more across this country and worldwide."

"Wordy, isn't he?" Gabby commented.

Damon shook his head, as he scolded her. "Shush!"

"There are simply too many of us to defeat, even if you had more than the two of you." The voice paused for a few seconds before continuing. "We have a better idea. Reconsider our offer. Join us. We had planned to use your vampire blood after Master DeVoie converted you. Even with your now Zompire converted blood, we're sure we could use it to make the vaccine Master DeVoie proposed to you. With that vaccine we can take over the entire world. We'd have an endless supply of blood for our needs from a willing population, all due to your original ancestral Dracula blood. The humans will volunteer their blood because they'll think it better to donate it than suffer vampirism, or death. You're the key to all this. You're a much closer descendent to Dracula than me, or any other vampire. Our scientist tried my blood...no good. It didn't work. We need you, Damon, and we think not Gabby. We need you...your blood...to make this work.

"Remember, you need blood too. We know you've substituted raw meat, something we can't do, but imagine having a population willing to give their blood to their masters...us...*you*. Imagine yourself as one of those controlling masters. Join us, and I'll even step down, and follow you to victory over these stupid humans as our new Master...*Master of All Vampires and Humans alike*."

CHAPTER 8

THE OFFER

Gabby placed a luscious piece of cow brain. She sucked any remains off each finger, one at a time. "Yummy." She examined all her fingers, but found no more brains. She gazed at Damon. "I guess he doesn't remember being human."

This time, Damon stared at Gabby, his gaze screaming, "Shush!"

"We've moved our headquarters several times to keep the authorities off our scent. In case you haven't found where our most recent headquarters is, come to Northwestern Connecticut, and set your GPS to Hunter Mountain. When you get here, call me at 888-555-8867, that's 888-555-VAMPire. See, we still have a sense of humor. Seriously, Both Of You, come join us. To fight us is futile, and stupid. Be smart, please!"

Gabby strolled into the room, licking her fingers again, enjoying the left over flavor. "Did he call us stupid?"

"Unintentionally, I think."

"There is nothing unintentional in what he said." She tilted her head, and snarled. "Come join us, and fall into our trap, You Stupid Zompire Couple." She straightened. "Once they've made the vaccine from your blood, they won't need either of us anymore. Then it'll be off with our heads. I don't know about you, but I'm kind of attached to mine right now."

Damon smiled. "Me too. I can't imagine what they're going to do with all their zombies. Can't have them eating the brains of our so called *willing* human donors."

"Maybe that's also why they want both of us. Maybe they want me to use my medical knowledge to get their slave zombies to eat something less devastating to the vampires' willing donors. Can't have the zombies eating their brains. Now can we?" She shrugged. "Who knows? I might win a Nobel prize in medicine for discovering a way to get zombies to eat animal brains like us."

"Or they may simply kill them all." He placed a finger against his chin. I wonder what happens if you give that same vaccine to a zombie?"

"That's one of the things I'm sure they would love to know, but remember what happened to the two zombies who bit you. They became violently ill. Apparently, a zombie can't tolerate biting a vampire, or, more precisely, a Zompire."

"I don't know about a typical vampire, but I *am* a direct descendant of the Count Dracula, the *original* Vampire. I always thought that was why those zombies became ill, too close to the original bloodline."

"Makes sense. In any case, you're not interested in their offer. Right?"

"Of course not. Despite their offer, I plan on destroying *every* vampire in this state, and then go state by state, if I have to, to destroy all the others. Dracula is an abomination, and all traces of his vampire progeny must be wiped off this planet."

Gabby frowned. "Present company excluded, I presume."

"You presume right. We can co-exist with the humans because we've maintained our humanity, even though it's cloaked beneath a combination of vampire and zombie bodies."

"And blood."

"Yes, *and blood*. We're different from those horrific monsters, and we cannot associate with them in any way except as their mortal enemies."

"Amen to that! Now, let's go collect Detectives Nolan and Beecher. I believe we need to convince them to join us in our Vampire hunt as our backup force."

CHAPTER 9

ZOMPIRE PLAN

Police headquarters bustled with unceasing noise. Drunken arrestees screamed their innocence and the police brutality that had occurred upon their arrest. Secretaries punched their keyboards. Many officers talked on phones.

Gabby and Damon, known to all the officers, were buzzed in as soon as they entered the police station, and strolled through this bevy of officers with no one taking note. When they arrived at Detective Nolan's office, they found him in a deep discussion with Detective Beecher. Damon knocked, and stood at the doorway. Both Zompires stood with wide smiles, awaiting admittance.

"Got a minute, Detectives?

Detective Nolan ran his hand through his long, sandy hair, using his fingers like a comb. His jacket remained open because of his plump abdomen. He smiled. "For you two, always! Come on in. Beecher and I were discussing your upcoming Vampire hunt. Running into you earlier today got me thinking of this worldwide vampire threat, Damon."

Beecher turned, and sat on the corner of the desk. Unlike Nolan, Beecher was tall and thin. He never tried adjusting his unkempt brown hair as Nolan had done. Both men wore blue pants and a white shirt, unbuttoned at the collar. "After you destroyed Vampire DeVoie, we've been expecting some kind of vampire, or zombie, apocalypse in revenge, but we've had no reports of strange occurrences anywhere in the state, no bites on necks, no brain eating zombies anywhere. We were discussing the vampire revolution, or whatever DeVoie called it. Does it represent a real threat, or simply empty words. We hate to close the case on that though, in case zombies and vampires suddenly start coming out of the woodwork, but it may be time to at least consider doing that."

Gabby sat in a chair in front of the desk. "Oh, that threat is real, very real. We had an example of that today." She proceeded to relate the events of the zombie attack at their home, and the message contained in the machete. She left out the part of her turning killer-crazed-zombie-destroying Zompire.

Nolan grunted. "Using a machete with a digital message! That's a new one. It's incredible. I thought vampires were stupid, and only existed to drink blood. I guess vampires *are* capable of using modern electronic equipment. Welcome to the digital age! Okay, the threat is real, and is coming to fruition. How do we combat it? Do we give all our officers sharp, wooden stakes with instructions to aim for their vampire hearts, and tell them to shoot all the zombie in the head?"

Damon laughed. "Not quite, although those things are effective against this plague. The problem is, we don't know how many vampires and zombies there are in their New England group, or worldwide. Arming the local police may be a very small drop in a very large demon bucket. We have a better idea. We're going to accept their invitation to join them."

Nolan nearly jumped out of his seat. He settled back into his chair. "What? Are you insane?" He leaned back, his desk chair squeaking, his face covered with deep furrows. "If you join them and become their f-'n President there's no way we'd ever stand a chance against them. You two are the strongest, craziest..." He searched for the word... "creatures...we've ever seen. Sunlight, wooden stakes, or machetes can't destroy you. You would be giving them access to a strength that the Human Race couldn't contend with in *any* way."

Beecher leaned over, placing his face in front of Damon's. "Listen, we know you aren't Superman and Superwoman, but you're pretty damn close. Why even consider joining them? After the episode with Vampire DeVoie, you said you had planned to start a Vampire War. You *promised* to destroy them, not to make the vaccine DeVoie talked about that would turn humans into willing vampire blood donors. We hoped you'd eventually come to discuss your plans to destroy that threat, not to tell us we're doomed, that our race is doomed, and certainly not to threaten us with extinction."

CHAPTER 10

TO KILL A ZOMPIRE

Gabby couldn't take the bickering any longer. She held up her hand. "Stop, Both of You! Stop panicking! We didn't come here for any of those reasons. If we were planning on double-crossing the Human Race, we would have simply gone to the vampire horde, and have done with it. We could have joined them as you now fear, and led them against you without ever telling you." She pounded her fist once on the desk. "No! We're here to seek *your* help and guidance in that Vampire War quest you mentioned." She shook her head violently. "We're not super heroes. No! We're simply a new…species…I guess you'd say, but a species that still appreciates being a member of the human race. Talk to Father Coulter, if you don't believe us. We still go to Church, receive the Sacraments, I'm in the Church choir, go out to eat with friends, and more. Of course, my menu choices have changed, and the restaurants we eat at know our preferences. They serve us rare steaks, or we abstain from eating at all when with friends."

Damon held up his hand. "Calm down, Gabby!" He leaned back in his chair, and took a deep breath before speaking. "We're all old friends here. We'd like to keep it that way. Unless we're mistaken, we're going to need each other in our quest, need each other very, very much. If we're antagonistic at the start, we're only adding to our chances for defeat. We need to act as a team, a team with a common goal of destroying all the vampires. We must use our forces together, and have each other's back. We need to act like surgeons, cutting out this vampire cancer."

Gabby grabbed Damon's arm. "Hey, that's my line! I'm the physician. I'll use the medical analogies, if you please."

Everyone laughed.

"Okay, Doctor Evans, tell them what happened to those zombies who attacked us."

Gabby lowered her head. "I destroyed them, each and every one of them."

Nolan tilted his head, and frowned. "That's a good thing. Isn't it?"

Gabby looked at Nolan. Her eyes filled with tears. "Well, yes. It had to be done, but it's what happened to me in the process that bothers me…us."

Nolan stared at her, afraid to say anything.

"I turned into some kind of…zombie killing machine, I guess I'd call it. They didn't stand a chance."

Nolan leaned on his desk. "Again, that's good. Right?"

She lowered her head again. She dropped her voice to a whisper. "I guess."

Damon wrapped one arm around her. "We're worried that the zombie part of us may emerge, and that we may become more zombie like."

Beecher leaned closer to her. "Sounds like you didn't have any control. Is that what I'm hearing?"

Gabby nodded.

Damon held her tighter, pulling her face into his chest. "We're afraid of losing all control, and becoming like them, brain eating zombies without any human feelings."

Nolan shook his head. "That will never happen! You're too strong."

"Maybe not. We don't know for sure, but, in case it does happen, we have a *huge* favor to ask." He paused, his gaze bouncing from detective to detective. "If it does happen, and you can't get us to stop attacking humans like mindless zombies, we want you to shoot both of us in the head. Incinerate us. Destroy our bodies. Burn them, and disrupt the resultant dust. We want no chance of resurrection."

"What? We could never do that."

"You may not have a choice. With our strength and Zompire abilities, we can't be stopped otherwise. We want you to promise to destroy us if it comes to that. You have to for the world's sake, for the safety of

41

every human on the planet." His gaze drifted to the floor. "Please. We beg you!"

CHAPTER 11

SPIES

No one spoke for several minutes. Finally, Nolan leaned back in his chair. "You're not kidding. Are you?"

"Not in the least." Gabby looked at Nolan and Beecher with tears filling both eyes. "You called us friends. You can't let us kill innocents, and risk destroying society, as we know it. We love it too much. We remember being Human. You've *got* to promise us."

Beecher and Nolan exchanged glances. Both heads nodded.

Nolan spoke first, and as quietly as he could. "Okay. We'll do as you say. We won't like it...we'll actually *hate* it, but you have our assurance that we'll stop you...destroy you, as you wish...but only if we deem you're not salvageable, a danger to society, as you put it." He lowered his head. "God, I hope it isn't necessary."

"We hope not also, but Gabby and I are resolute in what must be done. We will destroy all the vampires and their zombies, and take it from there, but we don't

43

want to add more complications to our existence, to *your* existence."

Nolan frowned. He couldn't say anything.

Damon nodded toward Gabby. "At the risk of upsetting Gabby again, we must remove this vampire cancer while sparing the Zompires, the good tissue."

Gabby sat bolt upright. "Hey! I resent being compared to tissue. I have feelings, you know." She smiled.

Everyone laughed. Damon stood, and closed the office door.

"Listen, now that you have agreed to what we asked, and we've calmed your fears…I hope…we need to discuss our strategy." He looked through the office windows at the other officers, busy doing their work. "I don't want anyone to overhear us as we discuss this further."

"You can't suspect any of our officers of being disloyal."

"Why not? The vampires must have got many of the police officers and politicians in their pocket wherever they've set up their headquarters. Otherwise, how could they have set up as many headquarters that Vampire Fabian bragged about? What's to prevent them from doing the same here? If they've planted a few spies out there…" He pointed to the officers outside Nolan's office… "Even if only one, and they get wind of what we have in mind, they'll be prepared for us, maybe set a bigger trap than they already have in mind. No, don't trust anyone out there, not even the Police Chief."

Beecher squinted. "Not even the Chief?"

"That's right. We're not going to be operating in his jurisdiction anyway. So, he doesn't need to know any part of our plans. However, I think we need *both of you* with us in this effort. You may have to request a leave of absence, or something like that, to be with us."

Nolan shook his head. "That's going to be difficult. We have a lot of cases we're working on. We can't simply take off a week, or two, or however long it takes. Some of those cases can't wait. We may be able to have them assigned to other officers, but that only works if the Chief goes along with it. I know which officers would work best. Those officers who have shown they are capable of handling the increase load without affecting their efficiency." He stared at Damon. "But the Chief isn't going to agree unless we can give him a very, very good reason…like vampire hunting."

Damon lowered his head to break the stare of Nolan. "Okay, maybe we'll have to trust *him*, but, if we do, we have to consider that the vampires may know our plans ahead of time, as if the Chief had told them. I'm sorry, but it's the only way we can assure our success."

Nolan shook his head. "Don't worry. I can talk to him, feel him out, and, if I think he's not connected to the vampires, I'll see if I can get him to agree to help us. I'll tell him the minimum, but, if there's a leak out there…" He pointed to the officers outside his office… "We may not know about it until it's too late, whether the Chief's involved, or not. The vampires may know we're coming anyway. So, forget any element of surprise."

"That's exactly what we were talking about, but we need you, and, if the risk of them knowing is necessary, we'll have to put up with that. We have no choice."

Nolan leaned on his desk. "OK, if that's settled, when do we start?"

"As soon as possible….maybe in a few days. We've got some things to collect, and plans to make. After we figure out where the vampires are located, you have to contact the local authorities in that jurisdiction to get permission for you to be acting there. We want them on our side, not acting against us because we're on their turf. The last thing we need is a turf war. We know we're risking a leak up there too, but, again, we have no choice. Let's tell them at the very last minute to prevent giving them too much time to think, or act."

"No problem. I have a few friends up North who owe me some favors anyway. They may be able to help us find their headquarters. I'll pull some strings, and see what I can do."

"Great! We have to be successful for all our sakes."

Gabby looked Heavenward. "Amen to that! Amen to that!"

CHAPTER 12

SUPERVISOR

Beecher held up one finger. "Before you leave, I have a question. If the vampires want you to join them, why send zombies after you? What kind of invitation is that? 'Come join us, but maybe these zombies will eat your brains, and bring us some of your blood.' Sounds pretty stupid on their part."

"You're right there. Gabby and I discussed that very point after the attack. I have two theories. Either, as you said, they sent the zombies to kill us, and collect some of my blood. Stupid, yes, but, if they had succeeded, and these new zombie-types could follow such a complicated series of orders, then, they wouldn't have to worry about us coming after them."

"Makes sense," Beecher said. "What's the other theory?"

"The Zombies overstepped what they were ordered to do. Maybe they were only supposed to deliver the machete, in other words, deliver the message, first by speaking to us, and then by machete. Maybe their appetites overcame their orders. So, they attacked us to satisfy their brain-hunger. In that case, the vampires were stupid to send even dumb zombies to do the job. Either that, or they were ordered to hand us the machete, and gave the *wrong end* to Gabby." He winked at Nolan and Beecher.

Gabby punched him in his shoulder. "Watch that, Mister, or I'll give you *the wrong end of the machete*!"

Damon rubbed his shoulder, as if it hurt a lot. "Won't work! You already proved that."

Beecher laughed. "Why use zombies in the first place? Shouldn't they have sent one of their own vampire members to deliver the message? Then, they wouldn't have even needed the machete-phone. A simple conversation would have sufficed."

"Remember I destroyed their last messenger, the one named DeVoie. Maybe they couldn't get a volunteer, or maybe it's part of their plan. Invite us, get us mad, and we blunder into their trap, all angry and unthinking. Whatever the reason, it doesn't matter. We have to plan our attack, and try to be prepared, as much as we can, for whatever trap they've set for us."

Nolan frowned. "Wouldn't they have been smarter to send a vampire *along* with the zombies as a supervisor."

Gabby sat bolt upright. "We hadn't considered that, but that makes a lot of sense. If we had agreed to go with the zombies, then they would have taken us to that vampire to start our journey to Fabian. On the other hand, if they succeeded in killing us, and I consider that laughable, they would turn over the blood sample from the machete to that same vampire supervisor." She tilted her head, snarled her lips. "Once we, uh, *I* destroyed the zombies, and after the machete delivered its message, why didn't the vampire approach us at home, or on our way here?"

Damon gripped her shoulder. He pulled her back into her seat. "Probably for the same reason Fabian didn't come himself. They're afraid of us, afraid of what we can do. Together we defeated DeVoie and all his zombies. They still don't know how strong, or how determined, we are. They need my blood, but are afraid of what the cost is going to be…maybe their destruction. It makes them sound afraid and very cautious."

Gabby's gaze shot around the room, landing on the window to the outside office. "That means we're right. There may, indeed, be a spy watching us right now, one of your *trusted* men, who we'd like to identify, if that's at all possible, before we move on to attack the vampire clan."

Nolan smiled. "Don't worry, that window is both soundproof and bulletproof. We've made this place secure from any terrorist attack."

"Still, he may have phoned Fabian about our response to the their message and the zombies at our home. Either that supervisor vampire, or one of your policemen spies, may be following us around to see what we do."

CHAPTER 13

VAMPIRE TRAP

Beecher rushed to the window. "I don't see anyone I don't recognize hanging around, and no one seems to be preoccupied by what we might be discussing in here."

"You won't," Damon said. "Any spy out there and any supervising vampire would be overly cautious. You won't see him, or her. I assume they won't know the details of any plan we may put into action, but they now know your department is involved, whether they followed us here, or that spy called about our arrival." He paused. "That means even more danger for you. They'll be waiting for us, but now they'll be expecting you too."

"Yeah, I kind of thought there would be danger. Now, there's even more danger, but that won't put me off. How about you, Beecher?"

"You've got to be kidding! I'm still here, aren't I? I didn't leave after that last scary encounter with a vampire and all those hungry zombies. I've no intention of backing out of this...what should I call it... adventure? No, I'm with you all the way. Besides, we have backup coming. Father Coulter and that nurse from the hospital…what's her name?"

Nolan snickered. "You must mean Marge Kerala?"

Damon smiled. "Okay, You Two Dedicated Vampire Hunters, and your incoming *backup*, let's get started with our planning." He turned to Gabby. "You met Father and Marge earlier. Right?"

She nodded. "I'm afraid they're coming with us whether we want them to, or not."

Nolan frowned. "Do you want me to order them *not* to join us? I'll command them as the police."

Damon shook his head. "That would only ensure that they would come…to spite you as the police. No, let's invite them to help us, and then, we can try to protect them too." He shrugged. "Who knows, maybe they'll be of some help."

Beecher looked Heavenward. "Yeah, right! Other than Father Coulter's cross that held back the vampire last time, I'm not sure what Ms. Kerala did."

Gabby said, "She protected the upper floor of the hospital from the zombies until Damon and I were able to disperse that zombie-killing gas."

Beecher nodded. "Oh, yeah. Now, I remember."

All turned toward the door, awaiting the couple's appearance. Father Coulter, dressed in his black Cassock with a large Cross dangling from a thick cord around his neck. Marge's large, African American body shuffled around the priest to enter. She wore a blue paisley dress that hung mid-calf. Her bright blue shoes completed her outfit.

Marge's gaze shot around the room. "Looks like you started the vampire hunting meeting without us. What's been covered?"

Damon jumped out of his seat, holding his chair so Marge could sit. "We got here only a few minutes ago. So, you haven't missed anything."

"Good. This zombie-destroying woman is ready for a fight. How are you all doing?"

Damon leaned against Nolan's desk. "That may not be necessary, Marge…and we're doing fine. We're glad you're here. We'd like your input on everything."

Beecher again looked Heavenward.

"Okay. What gives?"

"Did you hear about the attack on us?"

Marge nodded. "Yes, through the grapevine, via the police. My cousin works here. It's not a secret."

Damon said, "First, I'd like to intercept the supervising vampire who brought the zombies here, if, indeed, he exists. If not, we'll simply go onto the rest of our plan of finding them, and destroying them at their HQ."

Gabby turned in her chair. "And how do you plan to intercept the vampire, since we have no way of contacting him, or even know if he's in the area? Maybe through Marge's cousin?"

"Simple, we're going to set a vampire trap, using the machete. You did bring it with you, didn't you?"

"Sure. It's in the car, but how…"

"Let's get it, and sit in the city park down the street. Maybe he'll join us, if we look like we're trying to get the thing to work as a phone. Let's pretend the thing didn't work." He shrugged. "Let's make him curious. If the machete idea failed to give us Fabian's message, what's he going to report to Fabian…only that we destroyed his zombies?"

Gabby shook her head. "I don't believe you. You're setting yourself…no, us…up for another attack, this time by some freaking vampire."

CHAPTER 14

VAMPIRE SCIENCE

Nolan said, "We can help by surrounding the park. That would at least give you some protection. Maybe we can arm the men with stakes."

"No," Damon said, "that will scare him away. Remember, these vampires have heightened senses. He's sure to detect anyone who's there from the police. I want to flush him out, not drive him away. Besides, he could always change into a bat to avoid your men. That is, unless he decides to dine on a few of them before leaving. No, they would have no chance against a vampire. They're too fast, strong, and very deadly."

Marge turned toward Damon. "I'm in no mood, or shape, to fight a vampire, but if you plan to follow him, maybe Father and I can help. I've got my car out front."

Damon said, "Thanks, but still not a good idea. If he spotted you, he might stop to force you off the road, and attack you."

Marge pulled her head back, and pushed against the chair's back, trying hard to disappear into the seatback. Her full lips quivered. "A…a…attack me?

That's not a good idea then, not at all!" She squinted her eyes. "It was just a thought…not a good one after all. I defended the hospital against that zombie invasion, but that was with your zombie-destroying magic gas you invented."

Gabby smiled. "Not magic, but science that gave me that zombie destroying mist."

"Okay, then, *zombie science*." She puffed. "Unless you have some of that *science* to use on vampires, driving is out." She leaned forward. "Okay, driving is a bad idea. Let's move on. No more driving discussion. What's *our* next move?"

"Speaking of driving," Gabby said, ignoring Marge's question, "I assume the vampire transported those zombies to our home using a vehicle that would accommodate them, a van of some type. We have to assume he didn't carry them on his back as he flew here as a giant bat. So, he has a vehicle. Maybe we can find it, and track him in it."

Nolan reached for his desk phone. "I'll check any video surveillance cameras in your area to see if we can find footage of the car that carried the zombies to your home. Maybe we'll get lucky."

Beecher tapped the desk with his forefinger. "If we can find it, we can have our electronic geniuses plant some bugs on it, to make it easier to follow…GPS, and all that."

Damon stood, and opened the door. "Worth a try." Facing Marge and Father Coulter, he said,

"Detective Nolan will fill you in on what we discussed before your got here." His gaze shot to Nolan. "Maybe Marge's cousin can help you identify that…*leak*…we discussed."

"Leak? What leak? My cousin's a detective, not a plumber, nor a snitch!" She looked to the floor, and whispered. "However, if that's what you want me to do, I'll ask him." She looked up to Damon. "I can't give you any promises, though."

Everyone smiled.

Gabby rose. "Detective Nolan will explain, and yes, before you ask, you *can* accompany the police when we go after this vampire horde."

"Can't Father Coulter and I come with you?"

"No, we may have to change into a bat, or wolf to chase the vampire. You're better off, and safer, in a police car."

"As long as they have some way to destroy vampires in those cars, that's Okay with me." She looked to Father Coulter. "How about you, Father?"

Father Coulter rubbed his Cross. "May God be with us in this quest."

Marge looked Heavenward. "Amen to that! Amen to that!"

Damon held the door for Gabby. "Call me if you find anything, Detective Nolan. Otherwise, Gabby and I will handle our vampire visitor alone."

Gabby's eyes sprang open. "Visitor?"

"Sure. I don't want him on the defensive. So, I won't refer to him as anything negative, like our vampire attacker... until we spring our *vampire trap*, of course."

CHAPTER 15

PARK MEETING

After a 10-minute walk, Damon and Gabby sat on the green park bench closest to the entrance of Washington Park, the machete between them. They had a good view of the parking lot, and watched a few cars and vans enter. Several walkers passed, and stared at the machete, but no one questioned it.

Gabby sniffed the air. "Grass, flowers, fragrant roses, and one decaying body, covered in Musk. I guess he doesn't want to make a bad nasal impression when he finally appears. Ready?"

"Of course! I smell him too. My guess is he's in the parking lot, trying to avoid detecting, and deciding whether to come to us, or not."

"Probably smells our trap."

"No doubt, but if he's in the lot, he's at least curious. I think he'll show."

"I hope so."

Gabby licked her lips. "I'm getting hungry. Remind me not to attack him, and drain him dry."

"I wouldn't do that. It would make you sick, I'm sure." Damon smiled, and sniffed again. "I hope he shows soon so we can get him to tell us Fabian's plan. Then, you can destroy him, but only after we no longer need him." He shook his head. "But I still wouldn't drink his blood."

"I guess that's better than destroying him first, and never getting the information. That's for sure! Tell me, do we stink that bad?"

One end of Damon's lip rose. He leaned toward Gabby, smelling her neck. "You smell perfectly fine. As a matter of fact, I think you smell better than any perfume I've ever sampled on *any* woman."

Gabby narrowed her eyes, as she leaned away from him. "And how many women would that be?"

"Did I say *any woman*? I meant out of a perfume bottle, of course."

"Sure, you did! That putrid smell is getting closer. So, unless your body is suddenly turning all Zompire-vampire-zombie decaying *like*, the vampire is near."

"Good. Be ready for anything!"

Damon's cell phone rang. "Nolan here. The camera outside the park picked up a white van that just parked in the park's lot. That same van was seen in the vicinity of your home before the attack. Might be your *friend*."

"Thanks. We're still waiting on the park bench. While we're talking to it, have your men plant some bugs."

Nolan disconnected first.

A small bat then zoomed from the sky, landing in front of the couple. It morphed into a tall, 6 foot 5 inch, very white-skinned man, as if his body had *never* seen the sun. His blond hair looked disheveled, as if he had showered, but had yet to comb it. His dead eyes stared at Damon above a downward curved-tip nose, and lips snarled into a crooked smile, revealing his elongated incisors. With his fingers bent like an old, arthritic man, he opened his black cape, revealing a formal tuxedo, complete with white bowtie. Without taking his gaze from Damon, he bowed to the couple, never lifting his gaze from them. "Master Damon, Mistress Gabriella, I am the simple vampire, Enoch. I bear regards from Grand Master Fabian. He would have been here, but circumstances prevented it."

Damon raised his upper lip, exposing his incisors. He made sure his grew longer than his visitor's. "You mean he's afraid."

The vampire shrugged. "I am not familiar with his emotions. You'll have to take that up with him when you two meet."

Gabby sneered. The motion exposed one of her incisors, which she ensured grew longer than that of either man. "Before, or after he attacks us, and uses Damon's blood for his own purposes?"

Enoch squinted, and tilted his head, as he withdrew his canine teeth behind a deep, furrowed frown. He looked toward the parking lot. "What makes you think Fabian has any such devious purpose behind his invitation to join him?"

Gabby jumped to her feet, forcing Enoch to recoil. "Maybe because a group of ravenous zombies delivered his invitation via his machete. We had to fight them off before they ate *our* brains, and long before we got the message from him. Any other ridiculous questions?"

CHAPTER 16

ZOMPIRE MESSAGE

Damon stood, and placed a restraining hand on her arm. "It's Okay, Gabby. Enoch doesn't mean us any harm. Right, Enoch? He's simply a messenger from Fabian."

"Yeah, like the messenger zombies at our home? The message they gave us...*after* their attack, not before, I may point out... was much less cordial than it should have been. Are you about to attack us Enoch, and then give us another useless message?"

Enoch stepped back, placing his hands in a defensive position before him. "You're right, Master Damon...in a way. You see, I brought those zombies with me in case I needed them as a distraction for the police, and so on."

Gabby narrowed her eyes, as she yanked her arm free of Damon's restraint. *"And so on'* means in case we destroyed them as soon as we answered the door." Right?"

"Well...kind of. I was correct, in any case, since you destroyed every one. I watched from a far distance as you burned their bodies, Master Damon."

Gabby smiled. "I…well…we destroyed them because they attacked us. They announced their intention of delivering a message, then attacked me…big mistake. I destroyed them, which I intend to do to you, if you try a similar thing against us." She lowered her head, her gaze fixed on Enoch, as if she were staring above glasses. "So, don't try anything stupid. Understand?"

Damon again grabbed her arm.

Enoch bowed, this time allowing his gaze to fall to Gabby's feet. "I have no intention of trying anything, as you say, 'stupid.' As Master Damon said, I am a simple messenger. I have no grievances against you. I intend you no harm. As far as I know, Grand Master Fabian is sincere in his invitation for you to join us, to come to see our community, and hear what he has to say. Then, he plans to negotiate with you to prevent the misunderstanding that occurred between you and Master Vampire DeVoie. We're all on the same side. Honestly, it's us against the humans, and we'd like you on our side. That is what I understand of the message that Grand Master Fabian ordered me to deliver, anyway."

Damon sat, and pulled on Gabby's arm until she sat beside him. "Okay, Enoch, I'll be honest with you. I believe you mean us no harm. I further believe that the zombies attacked us because they misunderstood Fabian's instructions, or were driven by their zombie bran hunger, but I will be honest with you. I had intended to destroy you after meeting with you; however, I now believe you. So, I will not attack you. Besides, it makes no sense for Fabian to order an attack on us that he knows would be futile, and then have a prerecorded message delivered through that machete."

Enoch smiled, but did not move.

"So, here's what I propose. I'd like you to take *our* message to Vampire Fabian. Tell him that we will meet with him, but not at his headquarters, as he suggested. No, too many unknowns, and way too dangerous for us. We need to meet in a neutral arena. We'll get there, reconnoiter the place, choose the meeting place, and then get word to him through you. Do you have a cell phone?"

"Of course."

"Give us the number, and we'll call you when we're ready, but warn Fabian…no tricks, or else."

"Fabian will not take kindly to a threat like *or else.*"

"It's not a threat, not even a promise. It's a statement of fact. Take it, or leave it." He shrugged. "If he's so determined to meet with us as colleagues, and not mortal enemies, he's got to agree to our terms."

Enoch bowed again. "I shall convey your message. Here's my cell phone number. May I have yours?"

"Sure."

Enoch checked his surroundings, and found no one in the area. "He then ran at supersonic speeds toward the parking lot.

After Enoch had gone, Gabby turned to Damon. "I thought you were supposed to *destroy him*. I think those were your words. What happened to change your mind? I was ready to tear his head off, and would have except for your restraining hand."

"I suddenly realized we cannot destroy the vampires one at a time. Enoch didn't represent any real threat to us. He isn't our imminent, or ultimate, enemy. Vampire Fabian and all his followers, both vampires and zombies, are. We need to meet with him, and determine their strengths and weaknesses. We will then, and only then, attack, and destroy every one of them at the same time at their headquarters." He smiled, pulling Gabby closer until her head rested on his shoulder. "And then, I'll help you pull their heads off, and crush them like eggshells, if that's the way you want it in this vampire war."

Gabby narrowed her eyes, and smiled, as she watched Enoch, inspect his van, and then rip out something from underneath it.

Gabby sneered. "Enoch found Nolan's bugs."

"It figures. Should have known we couldn't fool him. I thought he'd want to fly back to their headquarters, not drive, but he's headed for the van."

The white van drove into the distance, moving with traffic to avoid standing out from the other drivers.

Thick drool drained from one corner of Gabby's mouth. "Like eggshells! Yeah!"

CHAPTER 17

ATTACKING FORCE

As Enoch's van disappeared around a corner, Damon stood. Gabby followed suit. She gazed at Damon.

"Now what?"

"Now, we follow him to their headquarters the old fashioned way, that's what."

"But don't we already know where their headquarters is. Isn't that what Vampire Fabian told us on the machete?"

"I suspect Fabian told us something so we could end up in his area, but he's too smart to give us the exact location. Enoch didn't offer that location either, but if we follow Enoch, we'll get their true location. Follow me."

Damon checked the area for passerbys, and then bounded high into the air, converting to a small bat. Gabby followed suit. They flew high above the surrounding buildings, searching the streets below for Enoch's van. When they spotted it, they slowed their flight, and climbed higher to avoid being spotted from below.

Two hours later, Enoch pulled to a stop before a bridge to a mountain, and spoke to two vampires. The side of the mountain slid sideways, disappearing into the rest of the wall of the mountain. It exposed a gigantic doorway. Enoch then drove through the opening, as the mountain door closed behind him.

Damon and Gabby flew to a nearby hill, covered with trees, where they converted to their human form. Both flexed their arms, and then stretched them above their heads.

Gabby turned to Damon. "The next time, can we follow in our car, or maybe take a commercial airline? My arms are exhausted."

"Mine too. There was no time to get our car, or book a flight. Sorry." He rotated 180 degrees. "Besides, there's no airport in sight, and the last few miles were dirt roads. Enoch would have surely seen our dust cloud if we had followed him in our car."

"So you think we were undetected?"

"I'm sure of it because Enoch came straight here. If he had detected us, I suspect he would have stopped somewhere else. Maybe call Vampire Fabian to warn him, and maybe set a trap for us. Besides, I didn't hear any warning calls from Enoch while we flew."

Gabby smiled. "Yeah, I like our super hearing. Just remember it, and don't talk about me behind my back."

Damon kept his gaze upon the closed mountain door. "Never! I know what's good for me."

Gabby became serious. "Now what?"

"Now we wait, and watch. That is, one of us does. I'd like you to go back to that town we passed a few miles back, and see if there's any indication of vampire activity there. Then, call our detective friends. Tell them where we are, and that it's time to get that paperwork rolling to give them authority in this community. By now, I'm sure they've found that their bug idea didn't work."

Gabby pulled out her cell phone. "Why don't I simply call them now?"

"I'm worried that Fabian might have tapped into our cell phones, and would hear the conversation, or could find us using the GPS chip. Enoch asked for our cell numbers, but that doesn't mean they don't already have it. It may mean they don't want us to know they have it. If we're right about that police spy, he could have easily gotten the numbers from our files. By the way, let's disable the GPS feature. Hope it's not too late. So, use a landline from that town."

Gabby disabled the GPS on her phone, and then did the same on Damon's. "Mission accomplished. Now, what do you want me to tell Detective Nolan besides the paperwork thing? Do you want them to get their vetted SWAT team members to this place, ready to attack the vampires, or what?"

"Not exactly! If they attack them before we know what their up against, too many SWAT team members will be killed. They're no match for a large bunch of vampires."

"And we are?"

"Maybe. We'll see, but I don't want to endanger the police unnecessarily. They're our backups, not the main attacking force, the one facing the first and largest danger."

"*Attacking...force*? What force? Are you talking about you and me, the Zompires, the only two Zompires?"

CHAPTER 18

MELDED PLANS

Damon nodded. "Yup, *if* I can come up with a workable plan, that is. I want the police here to maybe serve as a distraction, and maybe with a lot of wooden stakes for our final attack."

Gabby smiled, and slammed her hands against her hips. Her words came fast, almost non stop. "In other words, you have no idea how we're going to get in there, kill maybe a hundred, or more vampires, call the police in for clean up, and survive the whole affair. Right?" She squinted at Damon.

He blushed, and gazed at her. He then turned his gaze away. "That about sums it up. Have you got any other ideas? I'm open to all suggestions."

"No, not at the moment, but I didn't know I had to be the *Zompire brains* of this outfit." She tapped her temple with her right index finger.

Damon laughed. "You were always smarter than me. You know that. I believe we can do exactly what you outlined, but we need a workable plan first, and if we put our two heads together, I'm sure *we'll* come up with *something*."

Gabby looked Heavenward. "Oh, Brother!"

Damon grasped Gabby by her shoulders. "Look, Gabby, we both agreed that this vampire nest had to be destroyed. We've kind of located it, or at least got the vicinity right, and now we have to stamp them all out...permanently. Together we're stronger, faster, and, hopefully, smarter than the creatures in there. A plan will come to one of us but, if we put our minds together, we should have an *unbeatable* one that will save lives of both the police and the general public. What do you say? Are you ready for this fight?"

"As I always will be, I guess. Okay, Brilliant Zompire-Husband, how do we formulate this *unbeatable* plan?"

"Separately, I would think."

"I don't follow. Didn't you say we needed both our minds together first?"

"No! What I was thinking was this: while I stay here until dawn to see what activity occurs with our adversaries, and you're contacting the police, we'll each come up with a plan while we're separated. Then, when you return, we'll put our heads together, and meld the two plans into one giant, unbeatable plan. We can then figure the best time to surprise, and destroy them."

Gabby again gazed Heavenward. "Sounds a little hazy to me, maybe *very* hazy, but if that's the best the world's first Zompire can come up with, I'm willing to give it a try. What happens if you're discovered, or they move before dawn? How do I find you?"

"Then, you *can* use your cell phone. I'd like to keep the GPS off for now. Try not to call me unless I'm not here when you return, though. It's one thing to be outside the mountain, and be whispering. It's another to have a cell phone ring, or even buzz. That high a pitch may penetrate the walls, or maybe their sentries would hear it."

"Okay, I'll leave, and think of a plan while I'm gone. You be careful, though, and don't get caught by them. Remember, I will only have half of the plan. Who knows? Maybe I'll need your half to make it workable, but I don't want to have to rescue you in any case."

Damon chuckled. "Why not? That's a great plan in and of itself!"

Gabby frowned. "I'm off, but please be very careful. Those vampires are playing for keeps."

Damon whispered, "Yeah, but so are we."

Gabby jumped into the air, spreading her arms as she did so. She transformed into a giant bat that shrunk to a small bat, and flew upwards. Damon watched her until he no longer could see her, as she disappeared into the night sky.

Inside the mountain, Fabian dialed a number. It was answered on the first ring.

"Yes."

"She's on her way. Be ready for her, and don't take any chances when she shows up. These Zompires are a different type of animal. I don't want to hear she destroyed you. I want her here *alive*."

"Are you sure she's coming here?"

"Absolutely! Enoch heard them planning to follow him, and made sure they could. It's the way I planned it." He disconnected, and smiled, turning toward a TV screen above his desk. He watched Damon peeking around a tree. "Should have looked for hidden cameras, Damon. We're using the latest technology, as you should be. After all, we've got to protect ourselves from any intruders, including the all-powerful Zompires." He rubbed his chin. "Now, what will Damon do when we bring back his bride in a hearse?"

CHAPTER 19

POLICE STATION

As Gabby flew, she twisted her head to observe Damon, but soon he disappeared as she crested a nearby hill. She sighed, hating to leave him at the mouth of the enemy, but she knew the importance of her mission. She flew as fast as she could, her aching wings flapping nonstop the entire trip.

As the small town came into sight, she descended to get a better view of the layout. Spotting the police department, she dove to the alley alongside it. After checking for the presence of anyone who might see her transformation, she morphed into her human form.

After transforming, she spent a full minute inspected her clothes. She straightened her blouse, and brushed off some yellow pollen from her jeans. She shook her head, again wondering where her clothes went when she transformed into an animal, and mysteriously returned when she wished herself back to human. Finding pollen, twigs, barbs, and other debris clinging to her clothes had become the expected. She never could determine where, or how her clothes disappeared; however, she still hated how the transformation messed up her outfit and hair.

Shrugging, she headed for the front of the police station, determined to contact Detective Nolan. She climbed the six steps to the front door two at a time. She blasted through the front door, and headed to the policeman sitting behind the bulletproof glass at the reception desk. He had his head down, studying some paperwork. She knocked on the glass several times. His head snapped up.

He smiled, pressed an intercom button, and said, "May I help you?" He was young, clean-shaven, and had perfectly combed blond hair. His smile looked fake, plastered in place, with lips that barely moved when he spoke. The nameplate on the counter before Gabby read, "Det. James Lynch."

"Yes, I'm Doctor Gabriella Evans. I need to use your phone to contact Detective Nolan in Cantersville. He's expecting my call. It's kind of an emergency."

"*Kind of* an emergency? Is it an emergency, or not?"

"Well…okay, yes, it *is* an emergency. I need to speak to him immediately. Lives are at stake."

"Lives? From Cantersville, it's going to take them a few hours to get here to help you. Isn't there anything our local police force can do to help? After all, if lives are at stake, that's what we're here for."

Gabriella inhaled, and blew her breath out slowly. She shook her head. "No. It would take longer than that to have me explain all that has led up to this emergency situation. By then, if you even believed me, it would be too late. Detective Nolan will explain everything to you, or your superior, once I have him on the phone. So, I ask again, may I please have access to a phone to make that phone call? I don't know where else I can get a phone to make the call."

"No cell phone?"

"No, we left in a hurry, and I didn't get a chance to charge it. It's dead." She tilted her head and batted her long, red eyelashes. "Please."

Detective Lynch laughed, and leaned back in his chair. "Okay, I'll let you in to tell your story to our Police Chief. It'll be up to him to give you access to a phone. Before I let you in, may I see some identification?"

Gabriella huffed again, as she reached into her pants pocket to produce her driver's license. She slid it into the depression beneath the glass.

Detective Lynch studied it for longer than she thought necessary, and then, put it into a copy machine. "Have to make a copy for our electronic records to document your visit."

She looked Heavenward. "Do anything you have to, but please let me get to a phone pronto."

He returned her license, and pressed a button under his desk, that triggered a buzzer, and opened the lock on the steel door to Gabby's right.

"Thank you," she said as she rushed through the door.

Detective Lynch frowned, picked up the phone, and dialed an interior extension. "She's here. She looks pissed, and panicky."

CHAPTER 20

ATTACK

As Gabriella entered the main body of the police station, a police officer in uniform opened the door to an office. "Dr. Evans, I'm Police Chief Smithe. I understand that you want to call one of our colleagues, but won't tell us what it's about. Is that correct?"

"Essentially, yes. Detective Nolan asked me to call him when the situation here peaked, so he could join my husband and me. I'm afraid I can't tell you any more than that."

"That's Okay, Dr. Evans. I know Detective Nolan, and that sounds like him, but I'm going to give him Hell for not telling me about it first, so I could have been expecting your arrival."

"You can take that up with him soon, but, right now, I need to get on that phone."

"I understand. Please, use the desk phone in my office. I'll wait out here to give you some privacy, and will prevent any interruptions."

He held the door that opened into his office for her. She rushed pass him, and headed for the desk, located toward the back of the room.

He smiled as he closed the door.

She continued into the room, not noticing the uniformed officer standing behind the door. As she came into his sight, he pointed a gun at her.

Gabby heard a "puff" sound that occurred behind her.

The dart rammed into the back of her neck. She reached up, pulled the dart out, and turned toward her attacker, who loaded another dart into the one-shot weapon. She ran toward him, her eyes glowing fiery red, her incisors elongating with each step. Her skin turned white, as did her tresses. The door opened with a bang as it hit the adjacent wall. Chief Smithe aimed a handgun at her, and pulled the trigger. There followed another "puff." Gabriella put her hand up to stop the projectile. The dart dug into her palm. The uniformed officer fired again, this time the dart digging into the front of Gabriella's neck. She paused, pulled both darts out, and stumbled as the drug began to take effect. She collapsed onto the floor, her threatening gaze glued to the Chief.

Chief Smithe walked toward Gabriella's unmoving body, and put another dart into her back. Without taking his gaze from his captive, he reloaded his weapon. "Quick now, get the heavy chains to bind her. Let's get her into the casket." He fired an additional dart into the back of her neck. "Mustn't take any chances with this one…these Zompires are a different species, that's for sure. One tranquilizer dart usually suffices, not the four it took to take her down. Two more couldn't hurt to keep her that way." He pulled his cell phone from his pocket, and hit a speed dial number. "We've got her. She'll be on her way in a few minutes."

The disconnecting click was the only reply.

CHAPTER 21

IMPRISONMENT

Five minutes later, two policemen wheeled a silver metal casket into the Chief's office. Chief Smithe remained above Gabby with his tranquilizer dart gun pointed at her back, even though she hadn't moved. Another officer stood behind the Chief with another dart gun, pointed at Gabby's supine body.

Chief Smithe leaned back, but kept his gaze glued upon Gabby. "If she moves at all, hit her with another dart. Don't wait for any orders. Do it first, ask questions later. She is dangerous. Let's keep her unconscious…for now."

"But we don't know what the shock will do to her. Too much sedative might kill her."

"True, but I doubt it." He smiled wryly. "I can tell you one thing, however, if she recovers from all that sleep med, we'll all be in trouble. Master Fabian prefers her alive, but if she endangers us before we get her there, I want her destroyed…totally. To Hell with what Fabian wants."

"Okay, but it'll be your funeral."

"And if she gets through the extra dart meds, it'll be yours. Trust me!"

The officer shrugged, but kept his weapon pointed at her, nonetheless. The officers who brought in the casket opened it, and extracted long, heavy chains. It took both of them to get them out of the casket. The chains made a loud "clunk" when they hit the floor.

"Wrap her tight, make sure her hands and feet are bound tight to her body before you put her in the casket. I understand she's very, very strong, maybe even stronger than the casket alone. She could probably punch her way right out of it. I want those chains to keep her limbs from even attempting that."

The officers pinned her arms to her side with coils of the chain. They then continued the coiling around her trunk, her legs, and finally her ankles. Then, they took heavy locks, and bound the chain together at her chest and again at her ankles. The locks "clicked" loudly as they were closed.

Chief Smithe smiled. "Okay, that should hold her for the ride. Now, lift her into the casket, and then lock the chains inside to those braces on the sides and ends of the casket. The more locks, the better."

With one vampire at her head and the other at her feet, they bent down, and gripped her arms beneath her shoulders and her ankles. With an enormous effort they lifted her and the chain off the floor. They struggled to walk back to the casket, four other officers rushing to help in this gigantic effort. Suddenly, her left arm separated from her shoulder with a loud "snap."

One officer yelled, "Yikes! What did we do?"

Chief Smithe stepped to her side, pushing aside the officer who had yanked on her arm rather than the chains. "Keep going! Ignore what happened! Get her into the casket before she wakes. I hear these Zompires are part vampire and part zombies. My guess is that the zombie in her caused a weakening in her shoulder that resulted in the breakage, not something we did. We had to protect ourselves anyway, and bind her before we lifted her." A wry smile grew on his face. "Besides, it's only one arm. She has another."

With a trembling voice, almost a whisper, the involved officer said, "But what about Master Fabian. He wanted her intact."

Smithe growled at him. "He wanted her alive to use as bait for Zompire Damon. I'm not so sure *intact* matters so much! Get her into the casket, close it up, so we can deliver her to the mountain. I'll go with her in the hearse. You don't have to. I'll tell Master Fabian what happened. As long as she awakens after we get her to Master Fabian, she's his problem. If something happened to her once we closed the casket, he can't blame us." He let his gaze roam the faces of all the officers. "We all saw her put in the casket *whole*. She must have tried to get out of her chains, and the effort pulled her arm from its socket because of the zombie part of her. We all agree with that. *Right?*"

All the officers nodded, but no one uttered a sound.

"Good! Now, get those locks on those braces, close, and lock the casket, and let's get her started on her little journey. All of you stay here, and work as normal. Dawn's coming, so, as soon as you've finished with what you were doing, get downstairs and into your own caskets. I'll be back to join you before sunrise."

He walked out ahead of the casket. "You officers who've not yet joined our ranks need to cover the daytime shift as usual. Forget everything you've seen, unless you want us to attack you and your families. Remember, we'll kill you, but all your loved ones will become our slaves, and they'll remember how you betrayed them." His smile grew, but quickly turned into a frown. "Believe me, you don't want that! I've convinced Master Fabian to allow you few to remain to run this place during the daytime, but that will only last as long as I'm pleased with your work. You all can be replaced, if need be. Remember that!"

There were six officers outside Smithe's office who hung their heads. One said, "Don't worry, Chief, we all understand all too well. We'll handle everything until you get back tonight."

"You'd better! Lynch, you're with me. The rest of you, look busy!"

CHAPTER 22

SWAT TEAM PLAN

Detective Nolan signaled Beecher to enter his office with an enormous arm swing. "Have you heard anything from Damon, or Gabriella?"

Before answering, Beecher closed the door behind him, and then shook his lowered head. "No, and it surprises me. They came here to supposedly ask our help, and yet, not a peep from either one of them. Do you think that vampire they were going to ambush turned the tables on them. Do you think they may be in trouble, or worse, did they join him?"

"God, I hope not. If so, we've lost a very important ally, and with it, our only hope of destroying the vampires and their zombies."

Beecher took a seat, and checked his cell phone again. "Nothing. Do you want me to check their GPS to see where they are?"

"You can do that, but I don't expect you'll find anything. If they're way up in Northern Connecticut, I suspect they may not have good reception, and, if they've been captured, I'm sure their cell phones have been turned off, or destroyed…but check anyway. Maybe we'll get lucky."

"Luck aside, what do we do if we can't find them? Should we wait to hear from them?"

"Heck no! Doing that might turn out to be suicide for all of humanity and us. No, we go after them with everything we've got. It's our only hope, but maybe we can narrow the search by calling all the local precincts up there. But we have to be careful about those spies Damon worried about, even up there."

"That's easy to say, but it's going to be very hard, since we have no idea where they are. We'll be exposing our troops to vampires, zombies, and who knows what else, if we go traipsing around all the woods and cities up there, looking for vampires. I'm not comfortable with going there, wherever there may be, without Damon and Gabriella Drake as our allies."

"Me too, but we may have no choice." He leaned across his desk as he thought, and then said, "Tell you what, try to pick up their GPS signal, but don't make any calls to the local police headquarters until the sun rises."

Beecher leaned over the desk to get closer to Nolan. "And why not call them now?"

"As I said, Damon worried that there might be informers right here in our precinct. If that's true, imagine what we might find in some precinct we have no influence in. It could mean tipping off the vampires that we're on to them."

Beecher nodded his head, and turned to insure that no one was listening at the door. There were no listeners. "Okay, but how does waiting until sunrise help us? There may still be informants at those other stations. How do we identify the good guys?"

Nolan's gaze followed Beecher's around the station. "I'm not sure, but at least we'll be talking to human beings, not vampires, assuming they still can't stand the sunlight. After all, as Zompires, the Drakes tolerate the sun with no problem."

Beecher shook his head. "So, what are we supposed to do, call every station, and ask if they have had a problem with vampires? Those that don't will think we're crazy." He shook his head harder. "Hell, I'm not sure we're not crazy, anyway."

"No, we can't mention vampires, or suspicious deaths in their communities. We'll tell them we're looking for Damon Drake and his wife Dr. Gabriella Drake to help us with a case. Call them 'persons of interest,' but assure them they're not suspected of anything, and we only need to talk to them. I don't want anyone gunning for them, no accidental shootings if they find them."

"I thought they were immune to our weapons."

"They are! It's the police officers I'm afraid for. I don't want the Drakes forced to defend themselves. Good officers could be hurt, or worse."

Beecher nodded. "Understood. I think I'd better make those phone calls myself. That way, there won't be any errors."

"Do it from in here. I don't want anyone overhearing those conversations. My landline is secure. So, we don't have to worry about anyone listening in…at least by a wiretap."

"Eventually, you're going to have to tell our officers here, if you want them to come with us. You're going to have to trust them. They're well trained, and loyal. They'll surprise you with their dedication, but you've got to be honest with them. "

"That's what I'm going to be doing while you're making those calls at. God, I hope Damon is wrong, and none of our officers are turncoats. Once I let the cat out of the bag, I won't be able to keep our intentions from our general police population."

Beecher smiled. "I think you're going to be surprised by our men. They've been trained well…by you…and my guess is they'll be loyal to you and our cause all the way."

"Hope you're right. I'm going to start with the SWAT TEAM. Then, if we need them, I'll talk with the rest of the crew, all of them." He nodded at the door. "Now, try their GPSs. Maybe things will start on the easy side for us."

"Yeah, like every shift starts easy around here…never happened before! Won't be any different now! So, don't get your hopes up. *You-know-what* will probably hit the fan *real soon*."

CHAPTER 23

ACTING CHIEF LEA

A few hours later, Beecher rushed into Nolan's office. The SWAT team was there, discussing among themselves the craziness of what they had been told. All eyes turned to Beecher.

"Didn't find their GPS signal for whatever reason, and I never got the chance to check the stations up north, but you've got to hear what the Hunter Mountain Station has to say. The Interim Chief called, and is on line two. Put it on speaker."

Nolan didn't hesitate. He resumed his seat, and picked up his desk phone, punching the number two-extension button and then the speaker button. He returned the handset into its cradle, trying to be very careful to avoid any unnecessary noise. "Detective Nolan here. Detective Beecher said you have something to report. I'm here with our SWAT team. Feel free to say anything, no matter how crazy it sounds. We're ready for anything."

There followed a long pause. They could hear breathing, and, Nolan imagined the Interim Chief sweating, and trying to find the right words. He could wait no longer. "Chief?"

The female voice came through the speaker so low that Nolan had trouble hearing her.

"This is Interim Chief Longsouth." A long pause followed.

Nolan reached for the volume control, and cranked it to maximum.

"Listen Longsouth, believe it, or not, we will believe all you tell us. Crazy as it may sound. We've had a similar problem down here. We're ready to come to your help at a moment's notice, but you've got to tell us what your present situation is, and what you need. We need to know if you've seen Damon and Gabriella Drake. So, we're ready to hear it all. We're ready to listen to anything you can tell us."

"I'm…I'm the acting Chief. We've not seen this Damon Drake, but we have seen Gabriella Drake a little while ago." The voice trailed off to a long pause.

Nolan leaned closer to the speaker. "That's Gabriella Drake, Damon's wife. Is she all right? She had told us she would call us from up there. We haven't heard from her ever since. We're concerned. Please, Chief Longsouth, don't keep us in suspense. How is she?"

"She's alive…I think."

"You think?" The concern in Nolan's voice became palpable. "What do you mean, 'you think?'"

"Hold on, Detective Nolan." Her voice became muffled, as if she were covering the speaker with her hand. Only some words could be made out: "…get…car…fast. Call…there…us appraised."

When her voice became perceptible again, it shook, and the volume became even lower. Nolan reached for the volume button, and pressed it until it reached maximum to better make out all she said.

"Apologies, Detective Nolan. There's a lot going on around here."

"That's why we're talking. We knew one of the stations had trouble from both within, and without, and want to end that trouble pronto. We're here to help, but first we need to knows what happened to Gabriella?"

"Vvvvv….vvvvam…vampires! That's what."

CHAPTER 24

THE CASKET

Nolan leaned back heavily into his chair. "Shit! We thought that would happen up there somewhere, but were hoping we were wrong. Tell us your situation, quickly."

Her voice became stronger and steadier. "Hold on, again. Close that door. I don't want to be disturbed unless it's an absolute emergency that needs my attention."

A distant, "Yes, Mam," followed.

"Okay, I'm in the chief's office. So, we can talk freely, but I have to be careful. There may be…." Her voice trailed off.

"Informants, right?"

"Oh, yes. How did you know?"

"We've been warned about them in our own station. I had hoped it wasn't true. Guess I hoped in vain. What happened there, and what do you know about the Drakes?"

"You believe in vampires?"

"We have to after the incident we've had here involving the Drakes. They're not vampires, you know. They're Zompires, half vampires, good ones at that, and half zombies, good ones again."

"Yeah, we had heard those rumors. I guess the rumors were much more than rumors. Right? I understand the Big Wigs suppressed the full story in the press. True?"

"Oh, so true! The Drakes have been living in our town peacefully ever since they were converted. They were attacked by some zombies recently, and met with a vampire supervisor, apparently from up your way. We were supposed to go there together, to destroy those bloodsuckers, but the Drakes wanted to go first, and now they've disappeared. We can't find any trace of them at all." He leaned forward. "But for now we need to know what happened in your community." He shook his head, as if she could see him. "I'm through giving information until you fill us in on what happened. How we can help? So, tell us what happened, and what you need."

Her reply came without any hesitation. "Vampires attacked our HQ in the middle of the night a month, or so ago. They killed half the staff…I mean drained them *completely* until they became desiccated husks, really dead, not converted to vampires."

"Why only half?"

"They left the other half, us, the *lucky ones*, according to their leader, a vampire named Fabian, to

96

continue police work during the daylight hours. They keep us loyal to them by threatening to attack and kill, or worse, turn our relatives into vampires, or zombies, depending on how serious they decide our offense are. If we try to move our families out of harms way by sending them away, they've threatened to kill all of us, and hunt down our families to do the same things to them in any case. I never thought I would give in to such pressure, but all of us feel the imminent threat over our heads all of the time. We're all afraid to tell anyone outside the station, or call anyone for help."

Nolan's gaze drifted to Beecher. "And you're telling us now...why?"

A long pause ensued. "I can't see a happy ending, any good ending, to our situation without outside help. Your Zombie friend showing up here gave me hope that we might not be alone, and there may be others who might help us rid ourselves of this plague." She paused. "We don't know how to destroy all the vampires and zombies that infect our territory alone. I thought our only hope lay in some other Station, your Station, it seems, providing us outside help. The rumors up here say those same Zompires destroyed at least one vampire. They have the experience. I had hoped the rumors were true. Luckily, your Detective Beecher took my call, hoping to recruit some help. I really thought your Station would hang up on me when I said we needed help with vampires. I simply had to take the chance. We're despirate!"

Beecher said loudly, "You lucked out with that call. I happened to be passing an unoccupied desk when your call came in. Getting me was a good choice, Ma'am."

Her voice became weak again. "We'll see. What kind of help are you offering? How do we go about killing the already dead?"

"We're working on that as we speak, but, first, tell us about the Gabriella Drake."

After a long pause, she said, "She came here, asking to use our phones, something about her cell phone…no signal, dead batteries, or something like that. Makes no sense, since the signals should be strong, and she could have asked for a charger…."

Nolan leaned over the speaker, and yelled, "Chief Lea, damn the signal strength and charger! What happened to her?"

Her voice dropped, as she cleared her throat. "They carried her body out of here before dawn in a casket!"

CHAPTER 25

PLAYING DUMB

Detective Nolan's jaw dropped. He yelled into the phone's speaker. "Body? Casket? You mean a coffin…like for dead people? Was she dead? Was she *dead*? Is she…*gone*?"

Interim Chief Lea's voice faded to almost a whisper. "No, they anesthetized her with darts. God, it took so many darts. I don't even know how many. Anyway, she finally passed out. They shot her with a few more after that. I have to *assume* she was still alive at that point. They then wrapped her in heavy chains, and put her in a steel casket. I guess they took her to their hideout, wherever that is. We think it's in the nearby mountains somewhere."

Beecher buried his face in his hands. "And you didn't help her? You…simply watched her go down, and be taken away…like a helpless piece of…what…meat?"

"Well, if you put it that way, yes, but what do you think we could have done? We couldn't have stopped them. They're vampires, not humans. They're so strong. Our guns are useless. We don't have guns that shoot wooden darts to shoot at them through their hearts, and they wouldn't work if we missed their hearts, anyway. There are too many of them for us to use stakes and hammers. There's not enough of us…and besides we don't have any of those type weapons." She yelled, "What do you expect us to have done? Come on, tell me!"

Nolan turned a crooked eye toward Beecher. "It's Okay Assistant Chief. We understand, believe me." He snarled at Beecher. He hit the mute button. "Calm down, right now, Detective Beecher. Anger gets us nowhere." He turned back to the phone, again hitting the mute button. He tried to calm his voice. "But you need to understand, Interim Chief Lea, that we've lived with these Zompires for some time now. They have become…well, friends. In any case, they're our allies in this war we're planning against those same vampires. Hearing that one of them is hurt, upsets us…that's all, and tempers are short in this situation."

She delivered her response as slow as she could, her voice just above a whisper. "Yes, I understand." Her volume rose, as she asked, "What vampire war? This is the first I've heard of it."

Nolan nodded his head, as if she could see the motion. "Damon and Gabriella Drake came to us with a plan to attack those vampires in your territory, and destroy them." He then related the zombie attack on Gabriella and the message in the machete. "They gave us instructions to wait here, assemble a S.W.A.T. team

100

with those hammers and stakes you mentioned, and a few other surprises for those blood suckers. They knew approximately where their lair was because of the machete, but they then realized they were being watched by one of those vampires, and left here to trap him to get more information about the vampire hideout. We haven't seen, or heard from them since. Your information has provided us with the first hint of where they had gone."

"That explains why she came here then. Again, she came before dawn. That's when they took her."

"Was there any sign of Damon?"

"Not here. Maybe he's at the mountain, but if he is, he's way outnumbered."

Beecher leaned over the phone. "For now!"

CHAPTER 26

ANOTHER PLAN

Nolan again leaned back in his chair, thought for a few seconds, and then leaned forward to get closer to the phone. "Yes, you and Damon are outnumbered *for now*, but, as Detective Beecher pointed out, if we act fast, we should be able to help both you and our Zompire friends. We've got to get to your place before sunset. Is there any way we can kill all of the vampires infecting your station as they sleep…before they wake up at sunset?"

"I'm afraid not. During daylight, they lock themselves into the bomb shelter, located in our basement. It's a virtual fortress, built stronger than a World War II bunker, and designed to keep radiation out, as well as any invaders. Unfortunately that includes us."

Nolan thought for a second, resting one finger under his chin. "No problem, we'll get there today, before sunset, and set a trap for them when they emerge. We'll attack them, and destroy every one. I promise. Any other problems we can help you with, or equipment we can bring?"

"How about some lie detectors. I'd like to identify any spies among our ranks, who are not vampires, but may be working for them here at the station. If they get wind that we're going to attack them, they may get word to them via our phone connection with the bunker, or will let Fabian know what's happening here. We may never get them to come out, or may be swamped by more vampires from the mountain. Either way, we may be in for a lot more than we thought."

"You let me worry about that. I have a few ideas that may help. Is there any way you can cut those lines to inside?"

"Not without them giving them a warning. If I cut those lines, alarms will sound in the bunker, and they'll either come out to attack us, or at they might contact the mountain, and let them know we crossed them. If they stay in the bunker during daytime, and get help from the mountain at night, we're doomed. That's kind of what they threatened, anyway."

Nolan leaned even closer to the phone. "Oh, I think we have to believe them. They're smart and vicious. That's for sure. Okay, wait until we get there in a few hours. We'll attack that problem then. We'll bring our best electronic and communications men to help us...and we'll bring tons of weapons to use against them. I'm not so sure lie detectors will work on the undead, or on a human who's been brain washed into helping them. They may have no blood pressure changes, or breathing-rhythm changes, and so on, but it's worth a try."

"Okay, I'll wait, but I wish I could be of more help."

"Tell you what you can do in the meantime. You can try to find out who those spies might be. We have the same problem down here. What do you think would happen if you asked around the station for ideas on how to cut the lines, or maybe more about what happened to Gabriella? Act dumb, pretend to know nothing about cutting the line, and setting off the alarm. Tell all of your men you're trying to figure out a way to defeat the alarm, and maybe the vampires in the future. The ones, who tell you to forget it, and don't offer any solution, or tell you they'll think about it, are probably spies. Treat them like that anyway, but don't take *any of them* into your confidence. This trick may not work, or the spy may have a pat answer to make them sound innocent. We can't take the risk."

"Oh, I understand. It's a good idea though, and being the *Acting* Chief, I can play dumb, and ask what the real chief, before he became a vampire, would do. We'll see what kind of answers and clues I get as to who may not be on our side."

"Great. Don't do anything rash until we get there. When we do arrive, act surprised. We'll make up some believable story about why we're there…if anyone asks. The first thing I'm going to want to do is post a guard on that phone to the bunker and the doors to that basement. So, as soon as we get there, show us where those are. We don't want to give the vampires any forewarning."

"You got it. The phone is easy. It's in the Chief's office. I'll keep an eye on the door until you get here. I can see it from inside the Chief's office. Please get here as fast as you can. This Chief stuff is hard."

Nolan looked Heavenward. "Tell me about it! We're on our way, Assistant Chief Lea."

CHAPTER 27

TRAPPED

Gabriella stirred within the casket. Her head ached from temple to temple. She felt nauseated. "Strange, I never feel ill anymore. Where am I, anyway?"

She tried to move her arms and legs, but couldn't. She frowned. She tried to force her eyes open. They were stuck together with sticky matter, but without her hands, she couldn't wipe it away. They opened. Darkness. She concentrated on seeing in the dark. Her eyes glowed red, giving her surroundings a strange crimson glow. She found herself surrounded by satin material. She raised her head. A chain around her upper chest restricted her from rising farther. "What the heck? A chain? This looks like the inside of a coffin. Zompires don't need coffins. We sleep in beds."

She tried to move, finding it impossible, each move a difficult struggle. "Someone is determined to imprison me in this thing, whatever this *thing* is, anyway." A familiar noise filled her ears. "They've resorted to chains. Wow! First, I get shot with those damn darts from the police, and now, chains and what....a coffin? They've got to be kidding! They don't know much about Zompires. That's for sure."

By taking a deep breath, and moving her shoulders, she hoped to break the chains around her torso. Nothing. She found the same with her legs and feet.

"Tough chains. Okay, let's try a different approach." She tried to move her arms. "Something feels wrong! My right arm is pinned against my side. Why can't I feel the other?"

Lifting her head, she looked down toward her arms. In the red glow, she noted that her left arm was no longer connected to her shoulder. "What the heck? Where's my arm? There's no blood, at least none that I can see. It doesn't hurt either. What gives?" She continued looking around her prison. "Did they chop off one arm, and, if so, *why*?" She shook her head. "Maybe they wanted a Zompire souvenir. Dumb!"

She closed her eyes, and concentrated on her left hand. She tried to move it, as if it were still attached. She felt something at her left hip. She raised her head as much as she could again, resting it against the roof of the coffin. She could now see her left arm, and her fingers moving against her hip.

"Okay, this makes no sense, but let's see if I can control it to help me get out of here." She concentrated on her hand, trying to grip her pants. The fingers responded, as if the hand remained attached, and the orders from her brain flowed down still intact nerves. She pinched her pants, telling her arm to bend at the same time. The motion turned her arm around, inch by inch. Once the hand had climbed onto her body, she directed it to "crawl" up her torso toward her head, using her fingers as fulcrums against her torso.

"This is crazy! I don't believe it! At least,\ I'm in control of this thing. Okay, Baby Arm, come to mama's head."

The hand continued its slow crawl up her body, heading toward her head, finally crawling up her neck. She giggled.

"Never thought I'd be have my dismembered hand crawling across my face." She laughed. "I guess I've discovered a new way to scratch itches I couldn't reach before." She tried not to move her head, as her hand grabbed her skin. She turned her head a little to one side as the hand crawled up her chin, her cheek, her nose, her closed eyes, and, finally, her forehead.

"Okay, now to find my hairpin."

She felt behind her ear until she felt the cold metal. "I'm still amazed that I can feel things while my hand has no attachment to my shoulder. Ridiculous! Now, Girl, pull it out of your hair. Use your palm as a hinge. That's it. There! It's out."

She then reversed the hand's journey down her body, gripping the hairpin between two of her fingers. She managed the return trip with no problems, except it seemed to take a longer time. She finally arrived at the lock, linking the chain around her chest.

CHAPTER 28

ESCAPE

Gabby observed her hand's journey down to the lock that locked the chains around her with renewed amazement. *Don't care how this is happening, just that it is happening.* She spoke aloud, although mental commands seemed to be working as well. "Over to the lock! Now, I must remember what I learned in my wayward youth. Using a hairpin to open a lock is something I never thought I'd have to use to get myself free from anything like this."

She smiled. Grasping the hairpin between thumb and forefinger, she felt for the lock's opening, inserted the hairpin, and began a relentless turn, trying to get the lock to respond.

She slowed her breathing, hoping to decrease the noise in her chamber and the movements of her chest. "Now, what was it my cousin said about the tumblers? Oh, yeah, 'turn carefully, and listen quietly.' Should be easy with my super-Zompire hearing."

On the first deafening "click," Gabriella yelled, "Yes!" She then quieted, and stopped her hand movement. She listened for any change in the ambient noise around the casket. None. "Whew! I guess they can't hear me outside, wherever outside is."

She then continued fidgeting with the hairpin until the telltale "clank" proved the mechanism was unlocked. "There. Now to use my *free* hand…" she smiled at her use of the word *free*. It never meant so much to her as it did this day "…to pull the hasp out. Accomplishing this, she maneuvered the lock off the chain. She then wiggled her body, loosening the chain until she was free.

She picked up her "free" arm, and tried returning it to her shoulder. She sighed. "I hope it'll reattach." She shook her head. "I don't care if it even hurts a great deal. I'd like it back where it belongs." She felt no pain. Pressing the severed end against her shoulder, and holding it there for less than a minute, she noted the arm beginning to stick. A tickling sensation spread from her shoulder down to her fingertips. Tendrils of flesh grew from the arm and her shoulder, intertwining. Her arm tightened against her shoulder. First, her hand flexed close, and then opened on its own. Her arm bent at the elbow and extended without her input. She looked down at her limb. "Are you through moving on your own, now? I'd like control back."

She flexed the arm, placing the hand in front of her face. The red glow from her eyes made the hand appear like something from a Halloween costume. She smiled. "Okay, we're whole again. She kissed her palm. Thank you, My Now-Attached Arm. Now, let's see if we can get out of this coffin. I'm not ready for a permanent home in one…not yet, anyway."

She tried punching the satin-lined cover, but only dented the metal a small amount. She paused. "Wow! That's strong. What do I do next? Hope my jailer didn't think to wrap this casket in chains. I'm out of arms to donate to another attempt to escape chains and locks." She held both hands in front of her face. "Besides, they're both in here with me. None outside to undo the locks."

She placed her hands against the cover at the level of her waist, figuring its one catch and lock would be located there. She pushed. Nothing. She then pushed as hard as she could, wincing the entire time. "Come on, no casket-lid-top-lock should be able to stand a concerted push from a Zompire, especially a *female* Zompire with *two* arms no less!"

Suddenly, she heard metal shearing, tearing, and finally popping as the lid jerked open, striking the roof of the hearse. She held it there for several seconds while she peered out. Her red eyes again provided the only light. Shades covered the sides of the hearse. She pulled them back, and viewed the moonlit night scenery, whizzing by as the hearse made its way. Her eyes returned to normal without her doing anything.

She turned on her side, and crawled out of the casket. "Okay, now to make whoever is driving this van pay for restraining me!"

CHAPTER 29

ZOMPIRE ATTACK

By climbing on top of the casket, she crawled to its front. She found another curtain hanging from the ceiling, swaying with each movement of the car. She pulled it to one side. She peaked out, gazing upon the back of the driver and his passenger. Yanking the curtain back in one quick movement, she punched through the window with both hands. Shards of glass flew into the front of the vehicle.

Both occupants turned to the sound of breaking glass, until Gabby grabbed the back of their necks, and smashed their heads together. The hearse veered to the right, and sped off the road into the woods. When the hearse struck a tree mid-grill, both Smithe and Lynch flew through the windshield and onto its hood. Gabby thrust forward, but couldn't fit through the small window. Her shoulders smashed into the window frame. She then bounced back against the still-secure casket. She ended up on her back on the floor. She scrambled to her knees, and climbed over the casket to the back of the hearse. Now, using the red light from her eyes that had glowed brighter on the short journey, she found, and pushed, the rear door release button. Nothing happened. She punched the button again, harder this time. Again, nothing! She reached back, and punched the rear window. It smashed to millions of tiny pieces. She jumped out through the opening, looked upward, and screamed, the high-pitched scream of an injured bat.

Damon, still staked out at the mountain, several miles away, heard Gabby's scream. He stood, and searched his immediate surroundings for any danger. None. He jumped into the air, morphed into a bat, and headed in the direction of her scream. He flew as fast as he could, worried the entire time about Gabby's scream. *I'm coming, Gabby!* It took only minutes for Damon to cover the distance.

Gabby watched Damon's approach, as she leaned against the hearse, checking her fingernails for any damage. None. She glanced at Damon. A wry smile crossed her face. She brushed her hair back over her ear as if she hadn't a care in the world. This had become a motion Damon had grown to love.

He landed in front of her, examining her for any signs of injury. He found none that he could see. He then took several seconds to study the hearse and the two men ing unmoving on the ground. Turning to Gabby, he asked, "Are you all right? What happened?"

"The police attacked me. I guess they're all vampires, or at least they're on the vampire's side.

114

They shot me full of some kind of tranquilizing darts, and tied me with chains in there." She nodded toward the casket in the hearse. "Guess they've never tried to imprison a Zompire before."

Damon looked to the two policemen lying near the front of the van. He rolled his eyes, as he pointed to the men. "Sedated, tied in chains in a casket in the back of a hearse, and you still managed *that*? Impressive! Did you kill them?"

"Don't know for sure. I rammed their heads together, but from the back through that little viewing window I couldn't get enough power to crush them, bad angle and all." She raised her eyebrows. "Trust me, I wanted to." She lowered her head as she shook it. "I guess there are some limits to what I can do."

"Let me finish them for you." He took one step toward the vampires.

She grabbed his shoulder. "No! Wait! Maybe we can learn something from them, maybe use them to get into their hideout unnoticed."

"Okay, but let's tie them up with the chains they used on you before they wake up. What do you say?"

She nodded toward the vampires. "Be my guest. It's your job."

CHAPTER 30

THREAT

When Damon retrieved the chains from the hearse, he found the additional locks linking the chains to the braces on the sides and ends of the casket. He called out, "Honey, you'd better help me with these locks, or do you want me to just break them?"

"More locks? Hold on! Help me find my hairpin and I'll pick the locks. We'll use them to bind these two."

Damon smiled. "My wife, the thief."

"Be thankful for that education. It's how I got out of those chains in the first place." She decided not to tell Damon about her dismembered arm. *I wonder if I really am becoming more zombie than vampire?*

Using the chains, Damon tied the two vampires to a tree. He searched the area, retrieving two sticks that he whittled into points, using his pocketknife.

"You won't need those rinky-dink stakes. If they give us any trouble, I'll crush their heads, pull out their hearts, and set fire to what's left."

"Wow! They pissed you off like no one ever has that I know of, didn't they?"

She approached the two men with her hands on her hips. "I guess you could say that! Deep down inside I'm hoping they do get loose, or they do give us a problem…any kind of problem! I have it in for these two. They were in charge at the police station. Maybe Fabian ordered it, but these two implemented his orders. They're as guilty as him, maybe more so."

Damon raised his eyebrows. "Remind me again never to piss you off."

She smiled briefly as she knelt at the men's side. "Hey, wake up. I didn't hit you that hard." She shook them. Their heads flopped like bobble head dolls, but they didn't awaken.

Damon handed her a bottle of water he found in the hearse. "Here, try this. Seems to work in the movies."

She splashed their faces. They awoke soon after the water hit them. They tried to move, but couldn't. The noise of the straining chains informed them what bound them.

Smithe shook his head, and then stared at Gabby. "What happened? Fabian is going to kill you, Bitch."

Gabriella slapped his face with no warning. His incisors grew, as he snapped at her arm; however, she had yanked it back out of his reach as fast as she had slapped him. "You're too slow for that. Besides, we're both vampires…well, Zompires…already." She paused, looked Heavenward. "I should say Damon and I are *above* you vampires. You belong to the *old*

117

walking dead. Damon and I are *way* above that. We're not exact vampires, not exactly zombies, not exactly human, but whatever we are, we're better than you. We're stronger than you. We're faster than you. We're smarter than you. Your bite won't even hurt us. You're impotent as far as we're concerned."

"We'll see about that. Wait until you meet Fabian and all our vampire colleagues with their zombies. You can't destroy us all.   There's no way! You're outnumbered. You're doomed!"

Damon knelt down next to Gabriella. He shrugged. "That may be, but for now, we've reversed the tables on you. You're our prisoners now, and you're going to tell us a few things."

"Not on your Zompire-life! Destroy us if you want. We're not afraid."

Damon chuckled. "We didn't tie you up, and then wake you to destroy you. No! We seek information. If you'd like to survive this night, talk. If you don't, you'll stay tied up, and be roasted by the morning sun. It doesn't affect us. So, we don't care. My wife here would as soon see you roast as to get the information we need. It's all up to you." He began walking away from the vampires. "Come on Gabby, I've got something to tell you in private."

Gabriella followed Damon to the other side of the hearse. She whispered, covering the sides of her mouth with cupped hands. "Why'd you make me the villain back there? You wanted to destroy them as much as me."

"True, but it's the only thing I could think of at the time. We need to find a way to get in to their headquarters without alerting their entire clan that their enemy has invaded. I'm sure they're listening to us right now with their enhanced vampire hearing. But I wanted to give them some time alone to think about what we told them. Now, let's see what information we can get from them."

Gabby allowed her voice to bellow, "Then can we destroy them? Please."

"Wow, you've become a bloodthirsty Zompire! Haven't you, Mrs. Drake?"

"Let's say my zombie side is showing. I may tear their heads off to have a little snack on their small brains, but you talk to them first. Then, they're mine!"

CHAPTER 31

AGREEMENT

Damon approached the vampires with a wicked smile. "Now, as I was saying, talk, or be destroyed by the sun. It's your choice."

"You plan is to destroy us anyway. We can hear as well as you, Zompire. You plan to pump us for information, and then destroy us anyway."

Gabriella laughed. "Right you are, Chief Detective Smithe." She rubbed her chin. "I think I have a way out of this, however, that's both equitable and fair to all of us. First, you'll tell us how you had planned to get into Fabian's headquarters with me in the hearse, and then you'll deliver me to Fabian as the *guest* you had intended."

"Guest? We had you locked up, and chained. You were supposed to be cargo, not a guest."

She stood with a bent finger under her chin. "True, but all that has changed. I'll climb in the back of the car voluntarily. You can drive the hearse to Fabian's headquarters. That way Fabian gets what he wants, access to me and a proper introduction, and we'll get what we want, access to Fabian."

"You're nuts."

Gabriella shrugged. "Maybe, but whether I'm nuts, or not, you're still going to do what we say."

"And if we do?"

"Then you'll live long enough to witness my meeting with Fabian." She shrugged again. "After that, who knows?"

Smithe spit on the ground. "After that, you'll be dead. You both will be *really* dead, whatever that means for a Zompire. Fabian will destroy you with a stake through the heart, your heads torn off, or burned to a crisp…whatever it takes."

Gabriella smirked, and pointed at Smithe. "See, you've got the right motivation now. Don't cooperate, and bake in the sun. Do what we say, and live to see how nuts we are, and, maybe, just maybe, see your prediction of our *real* deaths come true. Again, it's your choice."

Smithe laughed. "You're nuts, but you also make sense." He thought for a short period of time, his gaze falling on his partner vampire. He returned his gaze to Gabby. "You're also right. You win. We'll get you to your desired meeting with Fabian without any problems. That way, we'll stay alive to see it and whatever happens afterward."

Gabriella strolled toward them, and reached for the chain behind the vampires. "Okay, I'll release you, but be warned. If you try to attack us,, or screw up our meeting in any way, we'll destroy you on the spot.

Believe me, two Zompires can destroy two vampires, namely you two, as easily as we all can morph into animals. I destroyed all Fabian's zombies alone. Damon destroyed Fabian's vampire DeVoie in that warehouse lair alone. So, don't try anything. Trust me, you can't win."

Smithe smiled, and shook his head. "Oh, I have no doubt about your abilities. Look what you did to us, and we had you chained inside a casket! No, we will cooperate…until you're with Fabian. After that, there's no agreement between us. Agreed?"

She smiled, and nodded. "Agreed. After that we can destroy you, and not feel guilty."

"That's not what will happen. You're the ones who'll be destroyed at the hand of Fabian, Our Ferocious Leader."

Gabriella picked the locks holding the vampires. She walked toward the hearse. "Whatever!" She beckoned the vampires with a broad stroke of her arm. "Come on, You Two. Help us pull the car out of the woods. You better hope it still runs, or we'll have to walk to the mountain."

"Don't blame us if it doesn't. You caused the crash, not us."

"Stop placing the guilt on me…at least until we know if it starts, or not."

Damon kept a safe distance from the three as they approached the hearse, ready to defend Gabriella if the vampires attacked.

They didn't, preferring to hold off any such attack until Fabian ordered them to destroy the two Zompires.

Damon then joined the others at the rear bumper. "Make sure you grab the frame of the car, and not simply the bumper. Otherwise, that will come right off. Reach well under."

All four grabbed the metal frame, and pulled toward the road. The hearse rolled back easily, its weight no challenge for strength of the living dead. After they stabilized the car on the road, Damon popped the hood. He inspected the engine and radiator.

"The bumper and forward frame took most of the impact. There appears to be no damage. It's surprising. It all looks good to me. Crank it over, Smithe."

The motor roared into existence.

Gabriella grabbed Lynch, who had remained quiet since the crash, by the collar. She dragged him to the back of the hearse. She opened the door, and tossed the vampire into the rear. "You'll ride with me. Get in the front on the floor, Damon. Don't want to warn Fabian too early. Can't do much about the damage to the car."

Damon climbed into the foot well in front of the passenger seat, and covered himself with a blanket he found on the floor. "If any of your vampire friends ask what happened, tell them some idiot cut you off, and you crashed. No one will doubt you."

"They better not! Is there anything special you want me to do as we approach the mountain?"

"Give them the correct password, if there is one, the first time, or I'll destroy you, and you won't get the chance to see our confrontation with Fabian. No tricks."

"Oh, don't worry. I want to see Fabian's face when you climb out of this hearse. I'm going to enjoy him destroying you two. They'll be no tricks from us." He gazed through the broken window behind his head. "Hey, Lynch, did you hear all that? Don't do anything to mess up the meeting. Let's live long enough to see these two utterly destroyed."

Lynch, kneeling alongside the casket, nodded his head. "Oh, I understand everything. I'm with you, Lynch. Drive on."

CHAPTER 32

NAIBAF

Damon spoke from beneath the blanket. "Drive slowly, Smithe. No sudden moves, or warnings. I really want to meet your Vampire Fabian without fighting my way in there."

Smithe remained silent. His gaze fell on Damon's cover. He didn't smile, nor make any movements that might indicate he understood Damon. After a prolonged period, he shook his head. "Don't worry! I'm resigned to our situation, and besides, I never break promises."

Putting the car into gear, he started driving slowly to determine if the steering still worked normally. It did. He then drove more speedily. As he approached the mountain, he slowed at the entrance to a bridge, guarded by vampires. He whispered toward Damon without taking his gaze from one of the guards. "We're approaching the first outpost. There's another one at the other end of the bridge."

Damon said, "Okay. Don't panic! We're all friends...for now."

As he slowed to a stop, a vampire advanced to the driver window. "What the heck happened to you?"

Smithe poked his hand out the side window to stop the vampire's approach. It worked.

"Something wrong?"

"No, but Fabian's waiting for this delivery. He would not want any delay. So, the password is *Fabian*."

The vampire backed away. "Okay, proceed, but, later, I want to hear what the heck happened to bang up the car so much." He smiled. "I thought you were a better drive than that, Chief."

Smithe forced a smile. "Yeah, that's what I thought until today. Tell you about it later, much later."

Damon shook his head. "'Fabian' is the password? Strange, but not surprising! His ego is immense."

"If you think that password is strange, wait until you hear the next one. It's almost a tongue twister."

Smithe drove slowly over the long, wooden bridge, crossing a deep chiasm. He glanced down once toward Damon. "Have to drive even more slowly over this bridge. Fabian told the guards that any vehicle that speeds across the bridge is an enemy, and to stop them before they make it across. I've always thought 'the slower, the better,' as far as this approach goes, anyway."

As they approached the mountain, the large door slid open. He drove through, but stopped soon after entering. Three vampires stood in front of the hearse, blocking its progress.

Smithe leaned out the window, although the broken windshield provided him an easy manner of conversing with the guards. "The password is *naibaf.* Fabian is waiting anxiously for this delivery. We need to see him immediately."

Damon covered his eyes, as he shook his head. "Naibaf?"

"Yes, it's Fabian spelled backwards."

CHAPTER 33

DELIVERY

As Smithe approached the large cavern inside the door, he waved at one of the two guards, standing on either side. Before leaning out his driver side window again, Smithe whispered, "Don't move, or make any noise, Zompire Damon." He smiled as the vampire approached, keeping his incisors small to keep his promise to not cause any problems.

"Good afternoon, Chief Smithe. You got her?"

"Yup. Fabian is waiting for her. I think he's going to be surprised at her condition."

From the rear of the hearse, Lynch mumbled, "That's for sure!"

Gabby leaned back, and delivered a kick to his shin. She said nothing, but shook her head, and "shushed" him with a finger to her sealed lips.

Lynch had all he could do to not yell out at the sudden pain in his shin. He moaned. He was surprised, as nothing had given him such pain since he had been converted into a vampire. *Man, these Zompires really can inflict more pain than the rest of us undead.* Although surprised, he said nothing aloud, but stared at

Gabby through red eyes. *I'll get you for that one, Zompire Gabby. I don't care who, or what you think you are. No one does that to me without reprisal.*

The vampire guard nodded toward the back of the hearse. "Who's that?" He leaned into the car, noting the broken window, separating the cabin from the rear. "What the heck happened?"

Smithe placed his hand on the top of the guard's head, and pushed him out of the car. "To answer your second question first, some idiot driver cut us off, as if we didn't exist. Anyway, I hit the brake, and the casket slid forward and broke the glass. It almost came right through the wall."

The guard's jaw dropped.

Smithe nodded. "I know, we should have tied down the casket somehow, but we were in a rush to get her here. So, we had the guys simply toss it in. My error! I'm sure Fabian will forgive me."

"*Only* if she's not damaged goods."

"We'll find out soon enough. As to your first question, Lynch is back there. He's pissed at me because he got tossed through the windshield when it all happened. I had a devil of the time convincing the other driver that we were unharmed, and we didn't need to report the accident. I almost attacked her, but was afraid that might draw attention to the both the hideout and us. Sure was hard to keep my vampire in check!

"Lynch didn't get hurt either, but it's going to take a long time for him to forget the incident...and to forgive me, even though it wasn't my fault." He tilted his head back, never taking his eyes off the guard, and raised his voice. "Isn't that right, Lynch?"

Gabby grabbed the front of Lynch's shirt, and cocked her fist next to her ear. She scowled at him.

Lynch's eyes bulged wide. "I…I guess. Anything the Chief says, I guess."

"If you want to see back there, go ahead, but I can't promise your safety with the way Lynch is at the moment."

The guard guffawed. "I think I'll pass. I'd love to see her, but I think I'll wait until Lynch calms down, and Fabian has with her. I don't want to upset Lynch any more than he already is. Besides, I'm not up to a fight right now."

"Good choice! *Your health* comes first."

"Ha! Okay, I'll let you in. Make sure Fabian doesn't destroy her before I get a good gander at her. I hear she's both good looking and a powerhouse. I like strong women."

"Oh, I don't think you'd like a demonstration of that power. She's much more than a powerhouse. That's what I saw at police headquarters, anyway." He shook his head. "You'd never believe it."

"Now, I'm even more intrigued." He turned toward the other guard who had migrated to touchpad that operated the mountain door. "They're Okay. Let them through."

The first guard stepped back from the car. "Okay, go ahead. By the way, you do know that Fabian's not here, right? Otherwise, I think he'd love to be here to greet you."

Smithe, who had put the car in motion, hit the brakes hard, pitching Gabby and Lynch forward. "What? He was the one who told me to deliver her here as soon as we had her. What gives?"

The guard shook his head. "Don't know. All I know is that Fabian tore out of here, flying North…some emergency up there, I guess. He took Enoch and several others with him. Don't know when he'll be back. You'll have to leave her here until he returns."

Smithe rested his head on the steering wheel. "Great. All this work, and he's not here." He sat upright, and turned toward the guard. "Let me go in a little farther. If I'm lucky, someone from upstairs knows what's going on. Maybe I need to take her somewhere else. I want her gone, and out of my care before she wakes up. Anyway, expect me to come right back out, in either case. I've got to get back to headquarters before sunrise to get into my casket. Thanks for the info…I think."

Damon stuck his head out from the blanket. "Listen, Smithe. Drive in, turn around, and drive out again. We'll get out where we started at the accident. I want to meet Fabian, but not all of his vampires at once, especially not before conversing with Fabian."

"Our deal still holds, right?"
"Maybe…I guess."

CHAPTER 34

GENTLEMEN'S AGREEMENT

Smithe drove carefully into the huge cavern hidden by the enormous rock-door. As he slowed the car, another vampire approached from the ramp that lead to the second floor. Smithe leaned out the window again, blocking the guard's view of the interior. "I hear Fabian's not here. Any idea where he is? I've got a delivery for him."

The vampire shook his head. "No one knows. He got a call, and flew out of here like he was being chased by the sunrise. Didn't speak to anyone. The guards said he headed north, but that's all we know. Took some others with him. Do you want to leave his merchandise here for him?"

"Better not. It's too important, too, too sensitive for us to leave it here. Might spoil. Who knows? Anyway, we'll go back to Police Headquarters, and await him. When he returns, tell him Smithe and Lynch were here with his delivery, and that we took her back to Police Headquarters for safekeeping. Have him call me with his instructions. Okay?"

The vampire nodded, and motioned to a vampire standing near the door. "They're leaving again. Don't close the door. Let them out."

Smithe turned the car around carefully, and then hit the gas. The tires spun before they finally gripped the ground, and the car jumped forward. It flew out the door, as Smithe waved a "goodbye" to the outside guards. He drove slowly across the bridge again. "I'm driving as fast as I can across this bridge, and I'm going to drive even faster to get back to where we met. I want you two out of the car before dawn for obvious reasons."

They arrived where they had begun their round-trip voyage. The car skidded to a stop on the shoulder. Smithe checked the side view mirrors, and leaned his head out the window to check the air above them. He turned to Damon, who had crawled onto the passenger seat. "We weren't followed. No cars in the area. Did you say, *Maybe* back there? Really? Are you going back out of your promise now because Fabian wasn't there? We trusted you. We did what you asked, without any problems. I expected you'd keep your promise."

Damon kept his gaze on the road ahead. "It wasn't a promise." He turned to face Smithe. "It was a gentlemen's agreement, nothing else, and you had no choice, really. Besides, you're no gentleman."

134

Smithe shook his head. "So, are you a gentleman, or a scoundrel who reneges on an agreement, *our agreement*, gentlemen's agreement, or not?"

Damon lowered his head, staring at him through his bushy eyebrows. "Well, if you put it that way…Okay, an agreement is an agreement…to be kept by both sides."

Smithe turned to see Gabby and Lynch seated in the rear. "But what about her? Do we have to worry about *her*?"

Damon sat back, his head hard against the headrest. "Maybe, but…don't worry! I can handle her…I hope." He shook his head. "I don't know exactly what's going on with her, but she's been acting kind of strange lately, really weird. I'm worried about her."

Smithe's gaze turned to Damon. "Yeah, like she went nuts destroying those zombies we sent to give you Fabian's message. If she does that again, this time against Lynch and me, please remember you're on our side, not hers…even if only on a temporary basis."

Damon held up one finger. "Only where it applies to our *Gentlemen's Agreement.*"

Gabby stuck her head through the opening, her gaze bouncing back and forth between the two. "Both of you…don't worry about me. Believe it, or not, I'm still more human than you and this poor excuse of a vampire back here. I'll do whatever I have to, including sticking to Damon's agreement…*any such agreement*…even if I disagree with its terms…as long as it doesn't interfere with my life, or our goals. So, you two are safe for now, but next time we meet, what happens will depend on the circumstances at the time, and whatever Fabian has in store for us. I'm not too happy with being shot with darts, if all he wanted to do was meet me, and discuss things, not happy at all."

Smithe turned to her. "You'll have to take that up with him. I just do what I'm told."

She scowled. "That's a cop-out, even from a cop! Anyway, let's get out of here, Damon. The rotten smell in the air is bothering me back here."

Damon opened his door, and turned toward Smithe before exiting. "Tell Fabian we came for a visit, but he didn't pleasure us with his company. So, we'll be back again. Have him call me when he comes back, and message me if he has to leave for any reason. We'll make sure we arrive when he's at home next time." He stepped out of the car, and then turned back to Smithe. "Oh, by the way, I don't want to have to sneak in next time. So, make sure Fabian lets the guards know they're to allow us in with no problems, and I mean *no* problems. Understand?"

"I'll give him the message. What he does with the information is up to him."

Gabby jumped out of the rear of the hearse. "Oh, we're aware that Fabian will have a few tricks up his sleeve for us, and not all good ones at that, but trust has to start somewhere. We stuck to our agreement with you to show you we're honest. So, we're offering him an Olive branch. Let's see what he does with it."

Lynch jumped out after Gabby, leaning away from her the entire way after landing on his feet. He ran to the passenger side, and jumped into the seat, slamming the door after him.

Damon pointed down the road, as he sneered at Smithe. "Get out of here before I change my mind, and turn Gabby loose on you."

CHAPTER 35

FUTURE AGREEMENTS

As the car sped away in the first dim rays of sunlight, Damon turned to Gabby, a deep frown growing on his face. *"Trust?* You know you can't trust him, don't you?"

"Of course, but maybe we can get his guard down a little. We need every advantage if we're going to find out what plans Fabian has for the Human race and us. Then, we can take steps to stop them, and then destroy all his vampire followers." She pointed to the retreating car. "And I want those two to be at the top of *my* hit list."

"Noted! They're all yours. You are getting *very* bloodthirsty and violent, Young Lady."

"No, I'm cautious. Fabian wants your blood for research, like DeVoie before him. That makes sense…to him, anyway. I do understand that, but Fabian already has a following. He doesn't need more vampires…or even Zompires…to follow him. What he needs, and what he wants, is your blood, your DNA to be exact. That is what *really* matters to him. He's hoping there's something in your original Count

Dracula DNA that his scientist can extract, and use to make a vaccine. If that's still the same plan as Vampire DeVoie voiced, that vaccine will convert the world's populace into an everlasting source of food for them. However, Fabian knows that we don't need that Human-volunteered-blood as food. We don't need any Human blood. So, why ask us to join him…beyond obtaining your DNA? Could he have another use for your DNA, something much more devious?"

"I can't imagine."

"Neither can I, but, we can't let your DNA get into his hands. If I'm right, and he has a new plan that involves needing our cooperation for some other wicked reason. We'd better find out what it entails, long before he enacts it, and way before either plan succeeds."

Damon nodded. "There's no way he's getting any of my Zompire blood for any of his evil purposes, whatever they are, voluntary, or otherwise." He shook his head. "After all, we're not bloodthirsty vampires! He has to know the world's populace has nothing to fear from us. We've said that often enough! We're on the side of Humanity…against *every* vampire in the world."

She scowled at him. "In that case, stop making agreements with the enemy. Remember, they *are* the enemy. We cannot, and should not, negotiate with them! We can't show *any* signs of weakness, or make promises that have the remotest chance of interfering with our ultimate goal…destroying every one of them. We've got to put an end to this vampire plague before it becomes whatever Fabian has in mind."

"I agree with you, but I still would like an audience with Fabian…to see if we can learn more about those plans, and maybe even discover all the vampire hideouts around the world. That would give us a direction to proceed after we destroy them all here."

She shook her head as she examined her fingernails. "We really don't need that information. Once we destroy Fabian, there's no one to carry on his evil research. Then, once we destroy his vampire group here, I'm sure the others around the world will find us, seeking revenge. So, we need to be ready for the onslaught of the vampires upon us Zompires."

Damon frowned. "That may be true, but it puts us on the defensive, and we don't know for sure that Fabian hasn't told another of his followers about his plans. That vampire may hide, and not attack us, but continue work on Fabian's plan. I don't want to have to be worried about that forever. I want to be able to attack those other vampires where they're hiding before they come after us, and before they institute whatever Fabian has planned. We have to destroy *every last one*, if we're going to be one hundred percent effective. If even one survives, that one will continue this vampire…" He paused, searching for the word. "…Infestation."

"Makes sense, but it all starts with us destroying Fabian and his followers first. Right?"

He nodded. "Agreed. So, let's not wait for his invitation. What do you say we go back to their lair, and break in this time? It's morning. They'll all be in their coffins. We can stab wooden stakes through their hearts, and be done with it."

Gabby shook her head. "You're forgetting one very important thing. Fabian and some of his troops weren't there when we were. Destroying only a few vampires accomplishes very little. We need Fabian and *all* his vampire followers."

Damon said, "Okay, then, we wait until nightfall to see if Fabian arrives. We then attack and destroy every one of them, before Fabian can establish another headquarters somewhere else. Agree?

CHAPTER 36

MAYBE...

She shoved her face to within an inch of Damon's. Her eyes glowed a brilliant red, casting an eerie light onto Damon's face, as if he wore red clown makeup. A copious amount of thick drool dripped from her mouth. She gripped both of his shoulders, and squeezed until Damon winced. She lifted him off the ground, and held him aloft. "I do agree, but in that case, no more agreements ...gentleman's, or otherwise. No more promises that I can't keep, or I'll destroy *all* of them on my own despite *your* agreement with them." She let him fall the one-foot to the ground, and then pounded her thumb on against his chest. "Believe me, *this* female Zompire can do that, or, at least, that's how she feels at the moment. Do you understand all that, Mister Zompire, Husband Of Mine?"

Damon stared at her, as if seeing her for the very first time, and became terrified at what he saw. He muttered, "I guess, but tell me, what has come over you? You singlehandedly *destroyed* those zombies." He glanced Heavenward. "Now, you're ready to take on the entire vampire nation…without my help. Have you gone insane, zombie crazy, or what?"

She smiled demurely. "Not one-hundred percent sure, but, somehow, I feel stronger than before. It's like I'm more than one single Zompire, more than the original human female I was, more than even you, and more than even Fabian and all his vampire followers put together."

Damon leaned back. "I believe you, but I don't understand that whole thing. Maybe we should have you see a doctor when this is all over, find out if your blood tests are out of whack, maybe you've got too much adrenaline floating around in you, or your thyroid is overactive."

She smiled. "Remember, I'm the licensed physician in the family. I only know of a few things that change a body like this." She thought pensively for a minute. Then, with wide-open eyes, she said, "Wait! Could it *be*?" She smiled, and looked Heavenward again. "Could it *really* be? Maybe! Maybe yes!" She shrugged. "Why not?"

"'Maybe what? Come on! Tell your non-physician husband. What could it be? "

"Never you mind…for now! I will take your non-physician advice though, and get some blood tests soon. I promise. Until then, you follow my commands, and only make agreements that *include* your Zompire wife's opinion, even if it disagrees with yours, and especially *not* with the vampire enemy. Understand?"

Without moving, Damon saluted, and clicked his heals together. "Yes, Ma'am!"

CHAPTER 37

HUNTER MOUNTAIN

Gabby shook her head, smiled, winked, and turned her back to Damon. "That's better, much better! Now what, Zombie Husband Of Mine?"

"Well, for one thing, I think we accomplished our quick visit to the vampire lair too easily."

Gabby spun on her heals, mouth agape. "Easy?" She squinted her eyes. "Were we in the same car, the one with two vampires, sitting with us, and the same mountain hideaway filled with vampires itching to pounce on us, or were you somewhere else?"

"Think about it. We expected to find Fabian there to discuss his so-called plan…for me. He shouldn't have known that if we got the chance, we planned to destroy him and all his followers. Of course, that presumes there were no vampire spies among the humans anywhere. What did we find? No Fabian, only some vampires, and probably the bottom-of-the-barrel vampires at that. On top of that, it seems to me we got out of there too easily. I think they wanted us to get in there, and then get out without being attacked."

"Why?"

He shook his head. "Not sure yet. It's not worth speculating *why* at the moment."

Gabby shook her head. "Okay, let's put that question aside for the moment. *We* weren't exactly invited in at that time anyway. Supposedly, they didn't know when we were both coming…*supposedly.* Wasn't their plan to have me delivered in chains to Fabian? If so, that plan failed miserably. If I hadn't managed to escape, he would have missed the opportunity to have me in his clutches. I'm guessing he had intended to use me as bait to get at you. What would he gain by not being there? Besides, how would Fabian know *not* to be there? Why do that anyway? We only came up with our plan to get inside his mountain lair, or whatever you want to call it, after the car crash. He couldn't have foreseen our *invasion* plan to meet him." She scrunched up her face. "It all makes no sense. He said he wanted to meet with *us*. He could only do that if he were there to meet *us*…well *me*, anyway. I still say his thought process revolved around you trying to rescue me, and coming to my aid. If so, he would get that meeting, and have you influenced by having me in chains. Why be away?" She shook her head. "I think you're overthinking what happened. You're not giving us, or more precisely, their fear of us, enough credit."

"That's it! He tied us up here while he was elsewhere doing…who knows what?"

"What would be more important than fulfilling his invitation to talk to him, and maybe capturing us to get at your blood?"

"I'm not sure. What else might be going on elsewhere, right now, and, if there is something, what has it to do with all this, and where is it?" He lowered her head. "I can't think of anything that might be more important to Fabian than obtaining my DNA."

She shook her head again, this time as slow as she could, and then put her crooked finger beneath her chin. "I have no idea either! Actually, nothing that I can even imagine....but maybe..."

"Again maybe? Maybe what? Don't keep me in any more suspense. I don't get it. What's gotten into you with all your maybes?"

"Well, we know Chief Smithe has been converted to a vampire. That's why he had the job to drive me. So, maybe Fabian figured you would rescue me before we got to his HQ." She smiled at Damon. "Of course, I didn't need your help. So, Fabian thought we would be kept busy...actually, we *were* kept busy...with Smithe's antics of driving us, while Fabian did some evil deed elsewhere." She turned away from him, and looked skyward. "That leaves so many evil possibilities for him." She paused, and then said, "Maybe there are many in that local police force that are still human. Those policemen would then be available to our police friends as our backup." She spun around to face Damon. "God, they'd probably love to help us! Fabian would want to be there to stop them from doing that, maybe even capturing, and interrogating the sheriff's human men before converting them to vampires."

"Why would he want to do that? What information could they possibly possess that he wants?"

"I don't know yet. Maybe he meant to find out more about our plans of attack from those human police. He may think they're in on our secret plans. Suppose Fabian and some of his vampires went to that town while we wasted our time with Smithe." She shrugged. "Who knows? It's only the beginning of an idea, but if so, they may be planning an attack on the police tonight, if it hasn't begun already. At the least, he could get any new information they might possess and more vampire soldiers for him to use against our forces."

"Weren't Detectives Nolan and Beecher supposed to follow us up here to help us? Maybe they figured out where we tracked Smithe somehow. Their bug didn't work, but Nolan's crew is very adept at their jobs. Maybe they figured it out. Wouldn't they try to make contact with those very human policemen in that town?"

"Oh, my God! If you're right, and they were able to track us, we've wasted a lot of very precious time. Our backup detectives may be rushing into a trap."

"We've got to get to that town, now, before it's too late!"

Both leapt into the air, converting into gigantic bats, and soared toward town.

CHAPTER 38

POLICE HEADQUARTERS

Detectives Nolan and Beecher, accompanied by 20 officers, descended upon Hunter Mountain like a horde of locusts. All eyes scanned the horizon, looking for the living dead. All of the streets appeared empty. Nothing moved.

Beecher turned to Nolan, "I don't like it. I know it's dusk, and I know we tried to get here during daylight, and failed...but there's no one in sight, no cars driving around, and all the shops, including the restaurants, are closed. They should be open. Where are all the hungry teenagers?'

Nolan scanned the area. "I'm afraid they're all still asleep in their coffins, but they'll be up any minute. I'm afraid. This may be a bigger task than we thought. I was hoping we only had to deal with the police who had been turned, not the whole town. We may not have brought enough manpower with us."

They parked outside the police station. The rest of the caravan lined up behind their car. Beecher exited the vehicle first, his head turning right and left, checking for any vampire headed toward them. "Eerie."

Nolan joined him. "You can say that again. Let's get inside before any vampires begin to stir out here."

The swat team chief approached them, his gaze bouncing back and forth. "I don't see anything. Where is everyone?"

Nolan answered, "Still in coffins, about to wake, I would think."

"I was afraid you'd say that. Wish we had gotten those crossbows with wooden arrows that I ordered before we left. We only had a few in the Station. They would be much more effective at range than these stakes we're carrying." He held up a 6-foot long wooden stake, sharpened to a fine point at one end.

Nolan shook his head. "Couldn't wait for them. Couldn't afford the time." He shrugged. "Sorry."

"That's Okay, my men will make you proud in any case. Vampires don't scare us. Bring them on!"

"Glad to hear that, but don't get too overconfident. These walking dead are very fast and astonishingly strong. Have your men use the longer stakes. Strike their hearts to kill them before they get too close. Remember they're *really* fast, so it may take two to three of your men to kill each one, one man to distract the creature, the other two to finish it off."

"Will do!"

Nolan headed toward the door to the Police Station. "Beecher and I are going in. Have your men stay out here. Keep an eye out for any vampires. Destroy them as soon as you see them. Don't wait for orders. Just do it." He shook his head. "If we don't come out to get you in five minutes, assume there's something wrong, and come in with those sticks blazing, so to speak."

"Understood."

CHAPTER 39

ACTING CHIEF LEA

Nolan and Beecher climbed the steps as if any noise would attract the vampires, followed by Marge and Father Coulter. Upon opening the heavy metal doors, they stuck their heads and torsos into the station. Several policemen worked at computer stations, unaware of the newcomers. Straightening up, Nolan and Beecher entered the station, again eyes searching the area for imminent danger. They flashed their badges to announce their arrival. No one noticed, until a female exited an office with a sign on the door that read, "Chief Smithe." Her eyes widened at the sight of the two detectives. She waved her arm, beckoning them to enter the office. She announced to the other officer officers, "These people are here to see me. I don't want to be disturbed."

She closed the door behind them. "Detectives Nolan and Beecher, I presume. Who are your friends?"

Nolan said, "This is Marge Kerala and Father Coulter. They were very helpful with our prior run in with that vampire and his zombies. They're here to help us."

Acting Chief Lea sighed. "I was beginning to fear you weren't coming…afraid something had happened to you along the way."

Nolan said, "Well, we were delayed, but we're here now, right on time, it appears. What's your situation?"

"Same as when I talked to you." She stared over their shoulders, her eyes wide, as if a vampire would suddenly charge into the room." She sighed, and returned her gaze to Nolan. "The vampires are still in their coffins downstairs. They'll be up soon, though. They wait a short period of time before leaving their coffins to ensure nightfall has arrived. The time they come up is never the same. They're smart, and really careful." She looked beyond the two men again. "Are you two alone?"

Beecher smiled. "No way! The swat team is outside, armed to the teeth with stakes."

"Hope that's enough. I've seen these monsters in action. They're so fast and deadly."

Beecher smiled. "We've planned for that, and have a flamethrower as backup weapon."

She frowned. "A flamethrower? That would be effective for a large number of vampires. I'd prefer you didn't burn down our headquarters, but, I guess if it becomes necessary…" She let her words drift into the air.

Nolan raised his hand, as if swearing in court. "Only if it becomes absolutely necessary. I promise.

Now, tell me about the town. Where is everyone? Are they *all* vampires?"

Father Coulter rubbed his Cross nervously. Marge made a hurried Sign of the Cross.

Lea lowered her head. "No. The vampires have consumed them for their food, draining every last drop of blood from most of them. I'm afraid they're all dead, truly dead. They've been drained dry. Who knows, maybe they're better off dead than roaming the night as the *walking* dead? They turned a few others into vampires, like our friends downstairs. That includes our Chief Smithe."

Beecher asked, "Why would they destroy the entire town's population? We figured they would try to keep a low profile, spreading their blood gathering over the entire State to avoid detection. Besides, they destroyed a ready source of blood for themselves. What they did screams vampire infestation in the area, and would call for some action for the surrounding authorities. Well, like it did with us. Sounds dumb on their part."

Nolan said, "Maybe that's what they wanted in the first place...our Zompire friends coming to save the day, and being vulnerable to capture. Don't know why, but it makes sense, anyway." He shrugged. "If that's their plan, it seems to have already worked on Dr. Evans."

Beecher frowned. "What about us? Do you think they wanted us here too for some reason?"

"I doubt it. They don't know we are the Zompire's backup…unless they do have a spy at headquarters."

Lea hung her head again. "Maybe *our* spy betrayed your planned arrival. If so, I'm sorry."

Nolan lightly gripped her shoulders, as she raised her gaze to him through tearful eyes. "We can debate that later, but for now, we've got to plan how to destroy them as they come up the stairs…before they can overcome us, and win this war before it has even begun." He turned to Beecher. "Go get the swat team before they come charging in here, and stab everyone in sight."

CHAPTER 40

THERMOPYLAE

Before leaving, Beecher turned to Nolan. "Seriously, what about the flame thrower we brought from my National Guard Unit?"

Lea's eyes shot open. She screamed, "Flame thrower, again? I told you, *no,* not in here! No way!"

Nolan smiled. "She's right. We can only use that outdoors, and only if it becomes our last resort."

Beecher nodded, and headed outside, sporting a grim expression.

Nolan again gripped Lea's shoulders. "Listen, I know this is hard, and I'm sure it's going to get harder, but, if we're going to end this curse, we've got to do anything we feel necessary."

Lea drooped her head. "I know. Okay."

"So, first, is there any way out of the basement besides that door?"

"No, there used to be a small window, but that was cemented over years ago to prevent anyone from squeezing through it, or planting a bomb right under out feet." She thought for a moment. "We have hot water heat. So, there's no duct work for them to fly through."

She paused again, and then shook her head. "No. That door is the only exit. What have you got in mind?"

"A trap. If my ancient history lessons serve me, the Greeks used a narrow pass at a place called Thermopylae to defeat the Roman army by forcing them through the pass in small numbers. In this case, we're those defenders, and this doorway becomes our narrow pass. They can only come through a couple at a time, and we can destroy them as they try to enter."

Lea placed her hand on her chin. "Sounds good, but after the first few are destroyed, won't the others turn into bats, or some other flying animal, and simply fly above us, or change into wolves, or other animals, making it harder to destroy individual vampires?"

Beecher entered bearing a large smile. "In that case, we'll use the flame thrower."

Both Lea and Nolan turned to Beecher. Simultaneously, they yelled, "No flamethrower!"

"I'm kidding."

Nolan shook his head. There must be another way."

Father Coulter held his Cross aloft. "I can be there, holding this Cross above me. That should repel at least some of them. Maybe we can delay them getting to us."

Marge rose, and headed for the door. "Unless that Cross keeps all of them downstairs, I think I should wait outside."

Lea pointed toward the ceiling. "Suppose we put garlic up there at the top of the door, and maybe hang it from the door trim. Wouldn't that make it more difficult for them to fly past it, and into the rest of the Station? If we then put the same garlic on the floor of the landing, that should slow their progress also…at least a little. I understand they can't stand the smell of garlic, and if they get close enough to it, it weakens them enormously. That's why they avoid it."

Nolan said, "Worth a try. Where do we get a lot of garlic around here?"

Lea scanned the room, as if gazing upon Main Street. "Not sure! There's none in the Station. They made sure of that after they took over."

Beecher leaned between the other two. "We passed a grocery store down the street. Maybe they still have some. I'll go check."

Lea shouted as Beecher headed out. "Break the door in, if you have to. We need that garlic. Get as much as you can carry."

Marge said, "I may make a dress out of it so no self-respecting vampire would even think of attacking me. I'll help round up the garlic in the meantime."

Beecher gave a 'thumbs up' as the door closed behind him.

Nolan waited for the door to close, and then said, "Now, let's get started positioning our men. God, I hope this trap works."

Lea looked Heavenward. "It had better!"

159

CHAPTER 41

"MAYBE"
THE FINAL REVEAL

Damon and Gabby soared high into the air. Gabby led the way with Damon trying to keep up. Soon afterward, they approached Hunter Mountain Police Headquarters. Gabby dove toward the front steps, landing at their foot. She converted to human form, and looked up to Damon diving toward her.

Damon landed behind her, puffing as if he had run a marathon. He bent over, and placed his hands on his knees, trying to catch his breath. "Where did you learn to fly so fast?"

"I'm not sure. I never could fly that fast before. Something in me has changed. I guess."

"Whatever gave you the power to destroy all those Zombies by yourself also gave you superior flying ability. Right?"

"Exactly. I'm a little surprised, afraid and energized, but, I think, happy. I'm not so sure how to express it."

"Energized? You're like that bunny who never stops. Your batteries must be overcharged. You act that way, in any case."

"I guess you're right, but energized is not the name for it."

"Well, what is?"

"I've suspected for some time now, but didn't want to say anything."

"Why not? What is it? Are you feeling ill, or something?"

"Oh, no! On the contrary, I feel the best I have in years. I feel like I could take on the world."

"I don't know about the world, but could you maybe take me on, or, better yet, take me *into* your confidence. Please! I'm a husband who wants to know, who desperately *needs* to know." He stared into her eyes. "I love you. We can face this together, no matter what *this* is, good or bad.

"Well...maybe..."

He glanced Heavenward. "Oh, no! Not *maybe* again. That makes twice you've said, *maybe*, but refused to explain further. So, no more stalling! Talk! We agreed to have no secrets between us, but this thing is driving me nuts. Are you taking some kind of stimulant I don't know about? Are the female Zompires simply stronger than the males?

"More intelligent too."

Damon looked Heavenward again. "God help me! Okay, okay! You're more intelligent. I've known that all along. You have all the degrees, college, medical school, and so forth that I don't. That, I guess, proves you're more intelligent, but what about your increased speed and power? Where'd that come from? And don't tell me your grandmother. It's new, fresh, and it's made you even more deadly. What gives?"

"Until now, I wasn't one hundred percent sure, but now…" She paused.

"Now, what? And please don't give me anymore '*maybes.*' I'm worried about you."

She dropped her head. "Okay. First, you shouldn't be concerned…well, not too much, anyway." She raised her gaze to meet his. "I love you." She leaned against the door, as if all the weight of the world pushed against her. She smiled.

"Okay, I'll try not to be worried anymore. Go on. What's happening?"

"I'm not one-hundred percent sure what's going to happen, but…"

Damon slapped his hand against the side of his thighs. "Now, I'm *really* beginning to worry."

Gabby pushed off the door, and threw her arms around Damon. She planted a big kiss on his lip, and then held him at arm's length. "We'll have to celebrate later, now that I'm sure, but…"

"Celebrate? Celebrate what?"

She pushed him away tenderly. She smiled, trying to reassure him. "You're about to become a daddy, Damon."

Damon's draw dropped. He stood open mouthed. "Da...daddy? Me? You mean..."

Gabby turned toward the door, smiled, and opened it. "It sounds like there's a war going on in there. Get yourself together, Damon Daddy, and follow the lead of your child's mother." She took one step into the Station, and jumped into the air, wings springing from her shoulders, as she morphed, and flew into the fray.

Damon's smile lasted only a minute. His eyes opened wide, as a deep frown covered his face. He shook his head, and then ran after Gabby, jumping as he morphed his body to imitate her. "Wait, you're pregnant. You shouldn't be fighting in your *condition*!"

CHAPTER 42

THE TRAP

Twenty minutes before they heard the vampires climbing the cellar steps, Beecher charged into the Police Station, trying to catch his breath as if he had run a marathon. He carried one overstuffed bag by its handle and another under his other arm.

Behind him, ran Marge, carrying another not so full bag. "Here's all we could find. Fresh garlic…all of it…at least all the store had."

Nolan pointed to the cellar door. "Great. Break it up and hang it around the door and in the ceiling above the doorway." He allowed his gaze to fall on Marge. "Sorry Marge, there's probably not enough to make your dress. We need all of it for the Station." He looked to Beecher. "Get our officers in here with their stakes, and have them huddle around the doorway. We'll destroy as many of them as we can when the door opens. After that, we'll have to deal with whatever they present us with." He frowned, his eyes glued on the cellar door. "However, this is a fight we can't afford to lose. We're the world's first, best, and, right now, only defense. Let's give them Hell!"

Beecher tapped Lea on the shoulder. "I'll stand at the rear, ready with the flame thrower, if necessary."

Her stare spoke nothing but contempt. "Remember, if you use that thing, we're at the front of those monsters…and we're human…with human feelings. Don't use it…unless there's no other hope."

Beecher dropped his head, and forced a small smile. "I was joking, really. I know I can't do it…not with our crew in here too."

Nolan shook his head. "Not funny, Beecher, not funny at all. Get your stake, and you can be among the first to meet these things. Marge, you stand near the front door to the Station. Make sure you get a stake from one of our men. Father, you're with Marge." He turned his ear toward the door. "I think I hear them coming up the stairs."

The SWAT team set up a perimeter around Nolan, Beecher and Lea. The remaining human police personnel stood alongside Lea, awaiting her orders. Some braced their stakes against the floor, using their boots as stops. Others stood with the stakes ready at their sides. All braced themselves, ready to repulse the initial charge of the undead. No one made a sound.

The door began to open a few inches into the room.

A gravelly voice broke the silence. "You humans should realize we have superhuman hearing."

Nolan's finger shot to his lips, giving the signal for no one to answer.

"We need you police personnel to watch the Station while we sleep. That's your job. You knew police will be safe from our attack, if you agree to let us in there, and not have to deal with anything you think you have ready to meet us."

"Nolan repeated his gesture, and shook his head, indicating, "No."

"We'll give you a few minutes to decide. After that, if we don't hear from you, all bets are off. You'll all be attacked, and killed. After sleeping all day, we're very hungry, and would love to drink all your blood. It's your choice, though. Take a few minutes to decide, but not too long. We're losing our patience. So, hurry up! You really have no choice."

Nolan approached the partially open door, and stuck his six-foot long stake a few inches through the opening. He yanked open the door, and thrust his stake through the opening, hoping to spear the first vampire.

CHAPTER 43

CONFRONTATION

The door swung open a few more inches. It made no noise. Nolan's thrust missed the first vampire because it managed to avoid the deadly stake by vaulting out of the way, transforming into a bat, and soaring over Nolan's shoulder. Nolan jumped into the doorway, hoping to block the next vampire. He swung his stake like a shovel that he used to empty trash. It struck the second vampire in the chest with a loud, "*Thunk.*" The tip penetrated deep into the vampire's chest and through its heart. The vampire's horrific, pain-filled scream riffled through the air. His body suddenly dissolved into black dust. A foul stench wafted through the Station, nauseating Nolan, and almost forcing him to vomit. He swallowed hard, and jumped back, bracing himself for the onslaught of the undead he knew would be ascending from the vampires below. He wasn't disappointed.

Before they could attack him, however, stomach contents ascended into his mouth. He closed his eyes, pinched his nose, and swallowed hard again, the saliva mixing with his stomach acid, and burning his esophagus. The pain of hundreds of razor blades exploded in his stomach. He doubled over. Beecher pushed him to the side, causing Nolan to fall to the floor, his stake bouncing to his side.

Beecher jumped to the head of their forces. He thrust his spear into the second vampire's chest as the vampire jumped toward him.

"*Thunk*." The stake shot through the vampire's body, easily emerging out his back. "Aaaarrgh." His momentum pushed him farther onto the stake, and forced Beecher to the ground. The tip of the stake shot toward the ceiling, causing the vampire to slide down the stake a few inches before his body dissolved into black dust that drifted down toward Beecher.

As the dust settled on Beecher, he clamped closed his eyes and mouth. He held his breath, and rolled over, allowing the stake to fall to the floor.

The third vampire jumped into the air, sprouting wings, and ascended toward the ceiling. The smell of the garlic slowed the vampire. As it drifted downward,

Lea ran forward, and thrust her stake upward, striking the vampire. "*Thunk*." The stake emerged and hit the ceiling. "Aaarrgh."

Lea leapt to the side to avoid the falling vampire dust. Before she could point her stake toward the other vampires, one of them grabbed her shoulders, and forced her to the floor. Large incisors grew inside its mouth as it landed upon her. It forced her head to one side, preparing to feast on the blood coursing through the veins in her neck.

Other vampires jumped through the door, some taking flight, trying to avoid both the stakes and the suspended garlic. The garlic smell weakened the vampires, and made them slower, but they persisted in their effort to escape, or kill their adversaries. Most charged the defenders in this effort. Several moved slowly enough for the defenders to destroy. Their screams filled the station, as did their foul smelling dust.

The vampire numbers grew too large for the battle, and several avoided the spear tips by simply pushing the stakes aside as they approached. Most were able to pin the defenders to the floor, preparing to quell their blood-hunger.

All of the trapped police screamed at the approaching incisors. Marge stood behind Father Coulter, who thrust his Cross at the first approaching vampire. The vampire raised his arm to cover his nose, mouth, and eyes. Marge opened the door to leave the mayhem. She turned to run, and was met by a gigantic brown hawk with a cinnamon-red tail, screeching, and flying into the station. Marge sat against the open door, allowing the Hawk easy entry. She covered her eyes with her forearm, and began crying.

CHAPTER 44

INTO THE FREY

Some of the vampires that had turned toward the hawk at her screech resumed their downward descent toward their intended victims. The wind emanating from the mouth of Gabby-Hawk blew like a hurricane, and knocked some of the attackers off their intended victims. It forced the vampire trying to approach Father Coulter back even further. As Gabby-Hawk flew upward, she held her breath briefly, stopping her destructive breath. This allowed those victims to grab their stakes from the ground, roll to a seated position, and thrust them through the vampire's heart. One policeman managed to thrust his stake through the back of the vampire being held off by Father Coulter's Cross.

Multiple "Aaaarrghs" could be heard from those dissolving vampires. The dust blew throughout the Station, driven by the next screeching blast from Gabby-Hawk.

The remaining vampires abandoned their intended victims, and turned toward the now attacking Gabby-Hawk. She soared toward the vampire that had flown to the top of the door, and thrust its beak clean through the vampire's chest. It continued to soar through the vampire's disintegration dust, charging toward the next vampire at the doorway.

The Damon-Hawk paused at the door, watched Gabby Hawk destroy several vampires, and then screeched as loud as he could. He flew toward one vampire that was about to jump on Gabby Hawk's back. Damon-Hawk tore across the room at full flight toward the vampire, pinching the back of its neck in its beak, and dragging him toward the other vampires. Damon-Hawk swung the vampire like a rag doll, striking other vampires, forcing them to the ground. The police personnel took advantage of the mayhem, and destroyed the floored vampires with their stakes. Dust flew everywhere, obscuring everyone's vision.

Everyone that is, except both Hawks, who, with red eyes, could see with no problem through the cloud. They continued their destructive flights through the vampires. The few remaining vampires converted to bats, and flew as close to the ceiling as they could, desperately trying to stay away from the suspended garlic.

Both Hawks flew toward the floor, and morphed into their Zompire form. Gabby reached human for first, "Marge, get up and hold the door open. Let these two bats out."

Marge hesitated, but stood with the help of Lea. She held the door open.

Lea turned to Gabby. "What? We've got them. We're winning. We can destroy them now like we did their comrades. Why should we let these two escape now?"

"Trust me. I need them to tell Fabian what happened here. Please, let them go. There are only two of them anyway."

The two vampires descended, and morphed into their human forms of Lynch and Smithe.

Damon stepped in front of Gabby. "Smithe and Lynch! I don't know what Gabby has in mind, but at least listen to her before you try anything attacking us, or escaping. It sounds like she's going to let you go, anyway. So, give her an ear."

CHAPTER 45

ZOMPIRE PLAN

Smithe stepped forward. He pointed at Gabby. "Attack her? You must be kidding. She spared us for some crazy reason. That makes twice she's had the chance to destroy us, and passed it up. I know we may end up fighting each other eventually, but I have no problem listening to her right now. She's obviously has something special on her mind. What is it, Zompire Gabby?"

Gabby stepped around Damon, and grabbed Chief Smithe's shoulders. "Damn right I do." She turned her head toward Damon, keeping her eyes on Smithe the entire time. She smiled. "I'm pretty sure that you're right about our fighting someday, but not today. I need you to tell Fabian we want no more surprises, no more fights, and no more human fatalities in this community, caused by his vampires…or zombies until we have a peaceful meeting first."

"That's going to be hard. We vampires need human blood, and our zombies thrive on human flesh and brains. We can't survive on animal parts like you two can….You Half Breeds."

Gabby squinted, and snarled. "Half breeds?" She thought for only a second, nodding before speaking. "For now, that's correct, but I have a plan that might benefit all the Fabian's vampires, including you two. That plan calls for us to meet with Fabian during a truce when we can discuss that plan. Deliver that message. Can you do that?" She dropped her gaze to the floor. "Name calling not withstanding?"

"For sure! How do I let you know his answer?"

She turned to Damon, again keeping her gaze on Smithe and Lynch. "Call us on Damon's cell phone, and we'll pick a place to meet…to talk. No funny business." She frowned. "It won't be pretty if Fabian crosses us again. He'd better be there. It'll be much worse than what happened here, if not. Got it?"

Both Smithe and Lynch nodded.

Damon pulled Gabby back. "Listen, Gabby's right. We're tired of being jerked around by Fabian. I mean, he orders Gabby drugged, and brought to his hideout, and then, he's not even there to accept the delivery. It made us think that he was manipulating us." He shook his head, and bared his teeth. "No, we were sure he manipulated us…for whatever reason. We thought he had come here to head the attack on the police station. We show up, and he's not here. Am I right? So, where is he?" He took a deep breath. "Don't give me that bull that you don't know what he's up to. You came here right after we let you go. Was he here when you arrived? Did you warn him to leave to avoid us again?"

Both vampires shook their heads.

Smithe said, "I know you don't believe me, but we simply did what we were told: deliver Gabby to the mountain, and return here afterward. That's what we did. He couldn't have possibly known that Gabby would escape, not destroy us, and force us to bring you two to the hideout."

Gabby frowned. "Do you really have no idea where Fabian is, or what he's up to? That's hard to believe."

Damon said, "I'll bet he's up to no good!"

CHAPTER 46

TO KILL BATS

Smithe shook his head. "We really can't tell you where, what, or why. He never confided in us. Maybe he figured you'd rescue Gabby before we got to the mountain, and would interrogate us as you did. Maybe that's why he never told us. If we didn't know, which we don't, we couldn't give him away." He shook his head. " We have no idea where he might be, or his plans."

Lynch mumbled, "Maybe he went with a bunch of our vampire friends up north to secure more blood for the group. He's done that in the past."

Damon frowned. "I'm sick and tired of *maybes*. That's all I hear lately, maybe, maybe, maybe!" If he's done that in the past, and is doing that now, why kidnap Gabby? Why take her to the mountain? Why not be there when she arrived? Even if he did suspect I'd come with her, he and your *friends* would have largely outnumbered us. Maybe his horde could have captured us...me. I thought that was what he wanted...my blood. He could have had the meeting he said he

176

wanted with us. He invites us with a machete recording, and then, when we show up. He's not there?" He shook his head. "What he did makes no sense."

Damon pointed to the exit. "Get out of here before I rescind Gabby's offer, and have Marge close and lock the door."

Marge moved to block the door with her body. "And I'll do exactly that, if Damon asks. Believe me, it'll be hard to get through this woman's robust body...especially if I slam this heavy door, and put it between me outside, and you inside, being eaten by *my Zompire friends*."

Two police guards joined Marge in holding the door open.

Smithe smiled. "No need, Miss." He turned to Gabby. "By the way, that was brilliant using the Hawk conversion to attack us. Hawks and snakes are our sworn, natural enemies...I mean, besides Zompires, of course. Those other animals eat normal bats...I mean non-Vampire bats...wherever they find them. Never seen one eat a vampire bat though. Don't want to, either."

Gabby smiled, and pointed to Damon and herself. "You don't have to worry about these two Zompires eating you. We have much better taste than that."

Smithe didn't smile, but frowned. "One question though. How did you know which bats were Smithe and me in our bat form?"

She raised her nose toward the ceiling, and pointed to it. "I could smell you. I got your scents when we were together, and it's very specific and strong. So, as I flew through your compatriots, but I prevented the police personnel from getting to you with their stakes. It was easy for me, and Damon simply followed my lead."

Lynch jumped into the air, followed by Smithe. Before he totally converted into a bat, he said, "I knew you were smart, and would have a workable plan in mind. I truly hope your plan works for all our sakes."

Gabby growled as she watched the two bats fly soar into the night, she growled. "It had better, for your sakes."

Damon stepped up to Gabby's side. "I have to assume hawks don't spear the bats with their beaks. How did you know spearing them with our bills would work?"

"The answer to that is I learned a lot about animal bites in Med School, not specifically about hawk bites, but I did learn that hawks and snakes ate bats. Since you already proved the vampire bites don't affect you, and the taste of you makes zombies sick, I hoped that if I opened their heart with a Zompire-hawk's beak, it would kill them. After the first, I was sure, and you see the result."

"I wasn't sure what would happen before you did the first. So, I used my beak to throw the vampires I could reach to within reach of the policemen with stakes, until I saw how effective your beak was. We made a good team."

Gabby nodded toward the police. "*We* all did."

CHAPTER 47

<u>FABIAN</u>

In the woods far north of his mountain hideaway, Fabian waved his compatriots onward.

Enoch approached him with his hands on his hips, motioning the others to approach also. "What are we doing out here in the middle of the woods? Are we looking for humans to collect their blood for our clan of vampire bats?" His gaze searched the valley before them.

"Not exactly. Although we've executed blood-seeking raids before, I have another reason for having you accompany me. I wanted you to meest our scientists. You were the only one willing to accept the danger inherent in meeting the Zompires for me. I, therefore, thought I'd reward you with a look into our glorious future…your glorious future. Scientists have been working on my secret experiment here for months."

"Secret experiment? I thought everyone, including those damned Zompires, knew you were planning experiments on Damon's DNA."

Fabian smiled. "Not *that* experiment!" He nodded, and expanded his smile, exposing his long incisors. "Yes, that experiment is very important, and, with, or without Damon's cooperation, that will continue. Thus, the humans are doomed…beyond help." He grew serious. "Listen, Enoch, having the world as willing blood donors is not enough. I want more for we vampires." He drooped his head. "I want what those Zompires have. I want their strength, all their superior abilities, and, most of all, I want my future progeny to be able to eat and drink from animals the way humans do every day."

Enoch's gaze shot to Fabian. "Isn't that impossible! Damon has those attributes only because he inherited Count Dracula's DNA. I understand he is a much closer relative to Dracula than you. That DNA changed him into the Zompire he is after he was bitten by both Master Vampire DeVoie and by a zombie."

Fabian smiled, and he pulled Enoch by his shirtsleeves down into the valley. "You're right. That combination was necessary for *his conversion*, but without those prerequisites would be impossible for anyone else. However, in this age where science reigns, I believe nothing is impossible." His smile returned. "Remember, his wife was human, and was converted after Damon bit her. That gave me an idea…an idea that will shock the world…I promise."

Enoch scrunched up his face, as he signaled the crowd of vampires behind them to follow by waving.

"I'm afraid I still don't understand. I've never heard of a Zompire being created before Damon. We're all descendants of Dracula in a way. I'll bet Damon's not the first human to be bitten by both a vampire and zombie, but no Zompire until Damon! He's different. He's a close, direct descendant of Dracula. It must make a difference. So, how will science overcome that, even with the correct DNA from Damon, combined with vampire and zombie DNA?"

Fabian stopped his progress, and turned Enoch to face him. He grabbed Enoch by the shoulders, and smiled. "That is my secret experiment, the experiment I designed. It's up to the scientists to carry it out, and produce my desired result." He let his gaze flow over the valley. "Come, and see what we've accomplished so far. You'll soon understand, and know your role in it soon enough. I promise you'll love it!"

CHAPTER 48

ENOCH

Enoch stared at Fabian in disbelief. "Me? What have I to do with all this? I'm *only* a simple vampire." He bowed. "Yes, I am your servant because you are my leader. What did I do to deserve such an honor? Meeting with the Zompires was a simple job, not something deserving of your attention, at least not to elevate me to the importance of being the subject of your experiments. The zombies took the risk, not me. I delivered them to the Zompire house. They carried your message. My job was an overseer, one there to assure they received your message, nothing more."

Fabian smiled. "Your modesty and homage to me is what has earned you this honor. Your trust is what I'm after. It's what I shall use to create *my* Zompires." He strolled toward the river at the bottom of the valley.

The river wound around the peninsulas that littered the valley. As they approached one such peninsula, Fabian stopped, and searched the surrounding woods and sky for any danger. He sniffed the air He could sense nothing out of the ordinary.

Fabian turned to Enoch. "If you ever come here without me, you must pull this branch down. The tree is real, but the branch is a lever. Watch."

As he pulled the branch down, a six-foot square opened before them in the forest floor. Dull silver, metal stairs descended downward into the dark. As they entered, lights illuminated their way." Fabian spoke as they descended. "If you ever come here as an animal, you still must assume your human form to enter. My scientists are working on some kind of *bat signal*, believe it, or not, that's what they calling it, that would work to open the hatch." His eyes drifted upward. "Apparently, one of the scientists loved the Batman series, and is calling it that." Fabian frowned. *Dumb ass scientist!* "I don't care what he calls it, as long as it works." His gaze returned to Enoch with a smile. "Don't worry about closing the hatch. Whenever it's opened, a signal is sent to the scientists. They will close it behind you." He pointed to a black semi-circular glass hemisphere on the wall. "That's a camera. They litter this place. The scientists are not worried about working with DNA, but don't want to be surprised by the humans, or Zompires." *Stupid scientists!*

Enoch smiled. "I can't say I blame them, especially the Zompires. I've seen them in action, and, man, can they move and fight with the best of us. They make us look like defenseless sloths."

184

"Yup, that's why I want our offspring to have those same abilities. We don't even know what other capabilities they may possess, or express in the future, but I want all of them."

As they approached a giant steel door with no apparent lock, it opened, and swung to one side. Enoch said, "I still don't get what my role in all this, not that I'm scared, or anything, but I'd like to know."

Fabian stepped to the side, motioning Enoch to enter. "The door opens automatically as one approaches. The scientists, however, can prevent the opening from inside, of course."

"They are really paranoid. Better safe than sorry, as the saying goes, I guess."

Fabian shrugged as he turned to the other vampires. "There's a waiting room, first door on the right. There's refreshments there…human blood…for you. Enjoy. Wait for us to finish. No one will bother you." He turned his back on them. "Enoch, you come with me. I want you to meet your destiny."

CHAPTER 49

SCIENTISTS

Fabian and Enoch entered the laboratory at the end of the hallway. Several scientists sat around granite top lab tables, handling test tubes filled with blood. Two stationed themselves in front of equipment for spinning the test tubes, and two were in front of incubators with the doors open. All wore protective face masks, and surgical gloves.

Fabian pointed at the ones working with the blood. "Those scientists are working on both human and vampire blood, but so far, their experiments have been a failure. Right?"

One of the scientists held up his thumb. "Right you are, Chief. We'll get it soon. Don't you worry."

Fabian frowned. "You'd better. Any progress?"

The scientist spun in his swivel seat. "We may have failed so far, but I didn't mean to imply we've made no progress. We have indeed!" He turned to the scientist in front of the incubators. "George there has taken the mixture we made of the two bloods, added some strengthening agents we know of from our former human science jobs, and will be incubating them for 24 hours. We think that should be enough, since most vampire transformations occur before that time period. Actually, from our records, the Zompire transformation took only a few hours, but Zompire Damon is, of course, different than the humans we used for our...er...your experiment. So, if no results in 24 hours, we'll stop the experiment, and call it a failure, but not until then."

Enoch frowned. *These are vampire scientists. Why wear the masks and gloves. They can't catch any disease from their subjects. Can they? I'd better not ask.* He turned to Fabian, and asked, "May I ask where the two blood samples came from?"

Before Fabian could answer, one of the scientists grinned, and stood. "Good question. One came from a human we drained yesterday. The other came from our imperious leader, standing next to you, our famous Fabian."

Fabian stepped up to the table next to the scientist. "Of course, my blood was freely donated. It felt funny to donate blood, and not simply suck it out of a human."

The scientist became serious. "We tried mixing human blood with simple vampire blood, and all it did was clot, even with our strengthening chemicals. Those are the experiments Fabian addressed as failures."

Fabian held up his hand to stop the scientist from further comments. "It was my idea to give my blood to the experiment. I'm a Drake, and closer to Dracula than any vampire on earth, except, of course, for Damon. He can track his ancestry all the way back to Dracula. My family is an off shoot, not direct."

Enoch bowed. "It was noble of you."

Fabian smiled. "Not really. I will do almost anything to move this experiment on. Donating my blood is a very small thing. You see, Enoch, those damned Zompires are closing in on us. Even with all the help of the vampires throughout the world, we may not be able to stop them. They are smart,, maybe smarter than us, and the female is a Physician. She used her medical knowledge to formulate a gas that destroyed DeVoie's zombies. They may figure out a way to destroy us. Before that happens, I want a way to get back at them. I want we vampires to control the world." He shook his head. "Humans have existed, and ruled, too long. It's time for us to take our place at the head of the table."

"And me?"

"Believe it, or not, you are the answer to our future. You represent the first step in our progress toward total control of the earth. You will be elevated to the stature of a *vampire-Zompire*."

CHAPTER 50

ENOCH, ZOMPIRE

Enoch stood before Fabian who he considered his lord and master. His eyes opened wider, and his jaw dropped. "Me? I've never thought of myself as anything more than a simple vampire, and, before that, a simple man. I'm not even a distant relative to Drakes, to Dracula. I'm nothing. I'm nobody. I am not worthy of any such honor."

Fabian smiled. "You're so humble. It makes what you will become even more impressive…to me, to your fellow vampires, and, above all, to the Drakes. You will destroy them! I will have my revenge on them for the destruction of Master DeVoie."

"I still can't believe my ears. Me? Destroy the Zompires? Unbelievable! Even if I had their power, there are two of them. There's only one of me, and those powers, assuming I get them, will be new to me. They've lived as Zompires far longer than I would have by then. That gives them the advantage. I have no idea what they are capable of, beyond what you've mentioned so far."

"That should be part of the *fun*. You can experiment here on the humans we capture and even on the vampires who volunteer for that. Several have already. They're like me in that they want the best for our species, and, if that means sacrificing themselves for our common good, they will do it without a second thought."

"Sacrifice? I'm not sure vampire should sacrifice themselves for me. I'm going to feel weird if that happens. Can't we do it in a test tube?"

A scientist rose, and walked to Enoch's side. "Some of the experiments will certainly be done that way. But field tests are the most important." He took his time walking back to his seat. "Even Fabian's plan to use the Zompire's DNA to make his vaccine will start in vitro, that is, in a test tube." He sat, and pulled a partially filled test tube from its holder. "However, even that serum, or vaccine, needs testing in the field, in vivo, as we say, to be sure it really will do the trick." He handed the test tube to his neighboring vampire. "That part of this experiment we can handle. We can collect the humans, and inoculate them, first to insure it's safe to give them. We don't want the vaccine to harm them. It's worthless if it kills any of them. After that, we'll proceed to giving it to a bunch of humans who we will bite after they're vaccinated to ensure they don't become vampires. If they do, that experiment will be deemed a failure, and we then recruit more vampire brothers and sisters." He turned toward

Fabian. "What Fabian wants is a good vaccine to *prevent* vampirization. If that happens, fine, but that only gives us a ready source of human blood to feed upon."

Enoch began sweating. He threw his arms out to the side. "I understand all that, but where do I come in in your experiment to make Zompires. I'm about as far from a Zompire as you can get."

Everyone laughed.

Fabian again put his arm around Enoch. "Your job in this experiment is simple. You'll let these scientists do any experiment on you they want." Fabian put Enoch at arm's length. "You're good with that. Right?"

"I...I guess so. What kind of experiments?"

The same scientist stood. "What we have in mind is to change your vampire DNA into Zompire DNA. That should give you all the powers Fabian has mentioned. Your new Zompire DNA will control your entire body. It should give you the Zompire powers."

Should? "But you don't have any Zompire DNA to copy from. Do you?"

"Not at the moment. Fabian has a plan to get some. Well, it's more than a plan. It's a trap for those Zompires. Assuming he succeeds, we'll copy the amino acid sequences in their DNA, and use some transcription RNA to institute changes in your DNA to match. And, presto, you're a vampire turned Zompire."

Enoch sneered. "I don't understand a single word of what you've said. I'm not a scientist. You've got to realize that."

Fabian gave him a small hug. "That's the point, Enoch. You don't have to understand. What they're proposing may be life changing, but we don't think it's going to hurt."

"Think? You mean they don't know! I'm willing to do anything you need done, Fabian, but I'd like to at least know what I'm in for. Pain doesn't scare me, but I'd still like to know ahead of time."

Fabian shook his head. "We don't know. No one knows. A total change in DNA has never been done before…to anyone, humans included. Trust me, these scientists are the best at what they do. That's why I turned them. They're now willing scientists working for me…for you…for us. I'm with you though. I don't understand most of what they say, but do know what they're doing. They'll have all the medications and resources necessary to treat any untoward reactions, or side effects."

Enoch smiled. "If you say so."

"Your participation is totally up to you, however. I picked you for this job because of who you are, and what you've done for us already. There's no shame in turning it down. If you decide that, the next on my list is Chief Smithe."

"Good man, well, vampire!" He looked down at his feet. "There's no reason to invoke him. I may not understand the steps, but I understand your plan, and agree with your goals." Enoch whispered as he nodded. "Whatever you want, Fabian. I trust you. I'll be your lab vampire-rat."

Fabian laughed. "Thank you. I think you'll never regret it. Now, if you'll excuse me, I have to return with our entourage to our mountain hideout. I go to prepare my trap for the Zompires that will lead to their total destruction and to our success!"

CHAPTER 51

COEXISTENCE

Damon approached Gabby. "I thought we weren't making any new agreements with the enemy. My highly intelligent wife made that announcement not too long ago." He puffed. "So, what are you doing, and what truce?"

Gabby smiled. "We need a temporary truce to see if we can get a better position for attacking them."

"You're not thinking of breaking that truce to attack them. That's more of Fabian's methodology." He frowned at her, and shook his head. "It shouldn't be ours. We shouldn't lower ourselves to his level of dishonesty. Besides, you promised Chief Smithe. I realize he's a vampire, and you want to destroy him, but you *did* promise…"

"Oh, I agree, and I would never break a truce with anyone, even with an S.O.B. vampire like Fabian, or Smithe." She shook her head. "No, if he agrees with my proposed truce, he'll get it. I really don't expect him to honor it, but in case he does, I'll present him with my plan for coexistence…a real plan."

Damon took a step back, as if retreating from a fire. "Coexistence? You must be kidding. I'm not interested in living next door to vampires that have attacked, and killed, many humans, including some of my friends. No, I'd rather kill them all…not live with them."

"I agree, but I want to give them, or at least Fabian, a possible way out. I expect him to turn me down, and use our meeting to try to destroy us at the same time." She tilted her head, gazing at Damon out of the corners of her eyes. "Of course, we are not going to allow him to do that. No way! If he does what I expect, you'll get your chance to destroy every one of them, including Fabian."

"Seems like a waste of time to me, and I don't understand your reasoning behind it, or why you're proposing it." He took a deep breath before saying, "but, if you want to give it a try, I'll back you all the way."

"That's good, because I don't think I can defeat them decisively without you."

"Well, thank you for that, but how about letting me in on your long-term strategy in case Fabian agrees with your *coexistence plan*?"

She turned to him, and waved the others in the room to approach her. "I thought you'd never ask. Okay, are you prepared to be knocked off your feet?"

Damon covered his eyes with one hand, and lowered his head. "Oh, Brother! Okay, we're listening, but I want to go on record again, saying how much I object to making any kind of agreement with *any* vampire, especially Fabian. So, okay, give!"

Gabby's gaze moved around the room. She saw expectant faces, awaiting her orders. They all gathered in front of her. These were the police, sworn to uphold the law, to protect the public. They had already risked their lives to eliminate the vampire threat to their community, and protect their fellow humans against a horrific brood. They had succeeded at the Police Station. She smiled, but then looked Heavenward. *I can't let them down, but can I convince them that my plan will work, that it must work, or will they see some ominous detail I've missed that will put them at worse risk? Here goes nothing, or should I say everything?*

Gabby took a deep breath before speaking. She let it out as slow as she could. "Okay, please listen to me to the end. This may sound a little crazy, but I think it's the only way we can succeed. If we *can* get that peaceful meeting with Fabian, I think we need to promise them our protection, from the police, we Zompires, the public…everyone.

CHAPTER 52

GABBY'S PLAN

Gabby spoke more quickly than she had intended. The jitteriness in her voice something she never experienced, but it became evident to all present. "Okay, now forgive me for not having all the details already worked out, but…"

Beecher covered his eyes with one hand as he shook his head. "Oh, no, she's going to give us half the plan, and we're supposed to figure out the rest, and then do the right thing, whatever that is. Typical leader!"

Damon stepped in front of Beecher, and pulled Beecher's hand from his face. "Okay, listen, we've survived thus far, including our first encounter with these fiends, based on Gabby's ideas, including those where she included only part of that plan. Let's give her the benefit of at least listening to her. Maybe we can then add to her plan, and improve it to give us the best chance of winning." He shrugged his shoulders. "If we don't, we're going into a hornet's nest of vampires without *any* plan." He shook his head. "That is not a very good idea at all."

Beecher smiled, his gaze drifting onto Gabby. "Sorry, Gabby! I guess leadership in our police has left me cynical. Okay, I'll listen, and hopefully learn how to survive our next encounter."

Gabby smiled. "No problem. I understand. We're all under severe pressure, especially facing the unknown. And that is where my plan begins." She let her gaze drift through the crowd, making eye contact with as many as she could. "First, we cannot take this first victory to heart. I mean that we cannot celebrate as if we've defeated them altogether. We had many elements working for us this time, surprise, a narrow entrance to this room, garlic weakening them as they passed it, and Damon and myself flying above the enemy, being able to eliminate many of them. On the next encounter we will have no element of surprise, no tactical narrow entranceway, no garlic, and we assume they will have a much larger number that we must meet. We'll have *nothing* working for us!"

Damon shook his head, and placed a hand on her shoulder. "Is this your idea of a pep talk? If so, it sucks!"

Gabby shook her head. "No pep talk! It's the truth. We cannot defeat them without planning. The vampires have everything working to our disadvantage. We've got to face that reality."

Nolan stepped forward. "I believe we all understand that, Gabby. So what's this offer you want to make to them? Won't that give us an even bigger disadvantage? Believe me, we know of your physical abilities, and I trust your judgment in most things. We'll give you everything you've said so far about our inferiority to the vampires. So, cut the excess talk. Get to the meat of that offer, and show us how we benefit from a *peaceful* meeting, and to agreeing to *protect* them from everything we believe in. I mean we've been protecting our society from vampires for years. I don't see coexistence working at all."

Gabby nodded. "Okay, but without that offer, I can't see us defeating them in an all-out battle. I was serious about offering them a peaceful solution." She shook her head. "I have no hope of that succeeding. From what I know about Fabian, he's smart, and he knows he has the advantage over our forces. He has both superior numbers and weapons…" Her gaze again drifted around the crowd…"those weapons being that all those vampires are so hard to kill, and are so deadly."

Damon placed a gentle, restraining hand on Nolan's shoulder. He stared at Gabby. "Let's assume you're right, and he doesn't take the peace offer. How do you think we can defeat them?"

"First, if Fabian agrees to our peace offering, we offer them not only protection, but supply them with all the blood they need to survive, after they pledge not to make any more vampires."

Damon shook his head. "Where do we get all that blood?"

"Blood banks. We tell the general public that some of the donated blood is going to nourish the existing vampires. Our next job will be to convince them that donating the blood to the vampires will keep that human population safe from vampire bites and deaths, I think that would be an easy task."

Damon shook his head. "I don't think so! Fabian will never agree to that. He doesn't trust us, or the general human population that hates vampires, and, like me, would rather see them all destroyed. He's demonstrated that distrust several times already." He frowned deep.

Gabby smiled. "Granted, but I think we need to be ready in case he surprises us."

Nolan dropped his gaze to the floor, and shook his head. "I can't imagine living in peace with those...those...vampires." He raised his gaze to Gabby. "Assuming he says, 'no,' how do we then fight them then?"

"It's risky, but we do it...by sacrificing Damon and me to them."

CHAPTER 53

SACRIFICE

All of the police cringed. Most moaned, "No!"

Beecher shouted, "You have to be kidding! Of course, it's 'No! It can't be anything else.'

Nolan shook his head. "You had better be kidding. We can't defeat these vampires without you. We need you at your best, not as some sacrificial victim to those bloodthirsty fiends!"

The shocked look on Damon's face faded as he smiled. "I hope you're kidding. If we don't destroy every one of those fiends, the vampires will still be after me, after my blood and my DNA, for their fiendish uses. I don't want to keep looking over my shoulder, looking for some creep with long teeth, a big syringe, or a big machete to collect my blood on."

Gabby held up both hands to silence the group. "Okay, maybe I chose the wrong word. I don't really mean we should be sacrificed to them, just *offered* to them. As we're assuming Fabian has already turned down our initial offer, I feel Damon and I should then go into the vampire horde alone, as if surrendering to them…with all of you ready to come to our aid at a moment's notice. The vampires may want to kill me to get me out the way. After all, what they want is Damon alive. That's why I believe the vampires captured me first, and tried to deliver me to Fabian. I figure Fabian was planning to use me as bait to get Damon to come to their mountain hideout to try to save me." She paused. No one said anything. "I figure one vial of his blood simply won't do. If the initial experiments to make a vaccine giving humans immunity to a vampire bite fails, they'll want more blood, and as Damon said, *more DNA*." She shrugged. "They know Damon and I are immune to vampire bites, as well as the bite of zombies. They must figure their scientists can transfer that immunity to humans." She shrugged. "Don't know if that'll work, or not, but we can't risk it. They want our immunity so much that I'm sure they'll fall for our sham surrender into their hands."

Damon snickered. "Our blood makes the zombies sick to their stomach. The zombies vomit all over the place. We don't know if humans would have the same response from drinking my blood…" he lowered his voice…"which I hope never happens for *any* reason…" he raised his volume to normal… "or what would happen from a vaccine made from my DNA. We may never find out. In any case, I don't know if Fabian wants sick humans in those that they immunize, or not, but it may be an unwanted side effect." He shrugged. "Fabian may not have a choice in the matter, and I'm sure if it occurred, no vampire would care how much the human population suffered."

Gabby nodded. "Damon will *pretend* to be captured by the vampires. That way defenses will be down, and we will have the element of surprise again."

Nolan held up a stopping hand. "Now, wait a minute. Suppose you are killed, and Damon is captured." He scrunched up his face. "I may be missing something here, but isn't that what we're supposed to prevent? If vampires capture Damon, they would have that unlimited source of his DNA. If we can't free him, we've lost...everything."

Gabby smiled. "I told you it was risky."

Beecher stepped forward. "And stupid! You can't depend on us being able to rescue Damon. We nearly failed with this small group here until you came, and mopped them up for us." He stared at Gabby. "And what about you? If you are killed, we've again lost the advantage before we even spring our trap...and you'll be dead. That's not risky. It's downright foolish!"

Nolan stood with his mouth wide open. "And stupid! No, that's a terrible plan, Gabby. I know you're smarter than we mere humans, but I agree with Beecher. What you propose is more than risky. It's untenable."

Damon allowed his gaze to fall to the ground at his feet. "Let's give Gabby a chance to *fully* explain her plan. I don't mind being captured by that group.

Hell, I'll even give them a quart of my Zompire blood…if we can destroy the vampires before they get a chance to experiment on it." He raised his gaze to Gabby. "So, as I said before, *give!*

Gabby smiled. "Damon's right. I have no desire to die at this time. I'll let the vampires capture me first…before Damon. I'm sure Fabian will then use me as leverage to get Damon to surrender. We know they can't kill us by the usual means used to kill vampires…stakes through the heart don't work and sunlight doesn't hurt us."

Nolan frowned. "But suppose the vampires shoot you in the head, or set fire to you, once Damon has been captured."

"I doubt that would happen. I'm counting on the fact that the vampires will want to keep me alive to use as leverage to get Damon's cooperation."

Nolan frowned deeper. "That's a *really* big risk on your part."

"Granted, but it's the only way to make them forget about the rest of our force. Besides, vampires are vampires. I doubt vampires have guns, or a fire arsenal. They have no need for either one, but I still say I doubt those would be used on me. If they are, I will fight like crazy to give you whatever signal we devise to come to our rescue…and kill our assailants the way you did here tonight at the Station."

Damon stepped forward, and shook his head. "No! It's much too dangerous."

Gabby turned to Damon. "Then, *you* come up to a better, safer, plan to kill who knows how many vampires, and do it very, very soon…like now!"

Damon frowned as deep as he could. *I don't believe my ears.* "You're serious, aren't you?"

"You'd better believe it, Oh, Husband Of Mine…very serious."

CHAPTER 54

FABIAN

Chief Smithe and Enoch morphed into Human form in front of the doors to their vampire cave, and nodded to the guards that had opened the door for them.

Upon entering, Smithe asked the interior guard, "Where is Leader Fabian?"

Fabian emerged from a room above, and walked onto a path that descended around the cave, ultimately ending at its base. "I'm here. What's up?"

Smithe hung his head. "The gig, I'd say."

Fabian frowned. "Explain, please."

When we awoke this evening at the Police Station, several policemen from another town and the two Zompires attacked us. They used wooden stakes, garlic and the element of surprise to destroy every one of us, except Enoch and myself. The female Zompire, Gabby, spared us to bring you a message."

"A message?"

"Yes, they want a meeting to discuss some idea Zompire Gabby has that she says will make both sides happy. I guess."

"Happy? You guess? I don't like the sound of that. I don't trust those Zompires. They're worse than fiends, they're our enemies." He put one finger beneath his chin. "They do represent our possible redemption, however, and a constant source of free blood, without the worry of stakes through our hearts from fearful citizens. However, Master Vampire DeVoie tried to get them to agree to a meeting with me after converting Damon Drake, and with what results? Immediate destruction of DeVoie and all his attending zombies." He shook his head. "No, it's got to be a trap. I can't believe they would now agree to a peaceful meeting...unless it's to trap us, to destroy each and every one of us."

"Smithe nodded. "As I said, they destroyed all our troops at the Station. We put up a valiant fight, but coming up the basement stairs forced us to enter the station slowly, say one or two at a time. They were waiting for us. When the Zompires showed, it was lights out for us. We didn't stand a chance." He drooped his head. "Zompire Gabby spared us. I can't tell you if they were sincere, or not. We're only the messengers." He let his gaze drift upwards to Fabian. He squinted. "So, what do you want to do? Have you got a plan, maybe a rebuttal to their so-called *offer*?

Fabian turned, and began walking up the ramp. "Not off hand, but give me a little time, and I'm sure I'll come up with something." He stopped half way up the ramp, and slowly tuned back toward Smithe. "By the way, thank you for attempting to bring Zompire Gabby here after you sedated her. Of course, I had planned to not be here, but I didn't think she'd escape that easily. If she hadn't, the ones I left here would have continued her sedation until I returned, and we could have used her as bait for Zompire Damon." He shook his head. "No matter. I'll plan a big surprise for them when they next appear, and then I'll use her to bait him to do my bidding. Anyway, did she give you any time line, or perhaps a place for us to meet?"

"No, no time limit, and no place for a meeting. I sincerely doubt that she'll wait too long, however. They seem very confident that they can meet with us, survive that meeting, and either get an amicable agreement, or destroy us. I think they may be overconfident after destroying our fellow vampire officers at the Station." He shook his head. "I've seen them in action. They are incredible...fast and strong...maybe faster and stronger than us. Their confidence is unbelievably high right now. It's like they don't believe they could possibly fail."

Fabian smiled. "Overconfident, yes! We might be able to use that overconfidence against them...get their defense down. Then, we can use Damon's DNA to make the vaccine that will make the rest of Humanity our everlasting supply of blood, and have them do it *willingly*. It'll be great." His smile grew as he threw his hands high above him. "Thank you, Zompire

Gabby, for coming up with the means to your own destruction at my hands. Thank you very, very much!"

CHAPTER 55

ATTACK PLAN

The return trip to the Station was quick, but quiet, no one wanting to break the uneasy silence. Gabby and Damon joined Nolan, Beecher and Lea in the Chief's office. Three sat in front of the desk, with Lea sitting in the Chief's chair. The other officers outside this office cleaned the debris left over from the destruction of the vampires. Using brooms and dustpans, they disposed of the vampire dust into garbage cans outside the Station. Finding a supply of cement blocks behind the building, they placed as many as they could on the tops of these cans, afraid the vampires would somehow revive, and emerge to attack them again.

Nolan threw his hands up. "I still think your plan is crazy, absolute crazy."

Gabby shrugged. "It's my life, and I'm the one at risk. If you can come up with a better idea, I'll listen. Fabian wants Damon, and I go along with my husband. I think Fabian now understands that…no Gabby, no Damon. So, we use that to get Fabian to agree to meet Damon through me. By me accompanying Damon, we have a chance of getting to a preoccupied Fabian, and surprising him and his vampire followers. We then have a chance of destroying all of them."

Nolan shrugged. "That's assuming he turns down your first *ridiculous* offer."

She shook her head. "Ridiculous? I must be the only one who doesn't think so." She shrugged. "I know if I were in his position, I would jump at it. Imagine, a chance to meet Damon on peaceful terms, a chance that could lead to a limitless supply of blood for them, no one hunting them down, no stakes through the heart, and the ability to live side-by-side with us Humans."

Damon snorted. "You've got to remember that Fabian is not as smart as you. He's a vampire, and has been changed from a logical human to a blood-seeking fiend. You recently called him smart. He may not be smart enough, or logical enough at this point, to see the advantages of your initial *offer*."

Gabby nodded. "That's why we need my backup plan." She stared at Nolan, and pointed to the officers cleaning the floors. "And that's why we Zompires need you and your men. They're brave. They proved that by taking on those vampires as they came upstairs, but the remaining vampires will have the numbers, as well as a strategic fortress behind those huge doors at that mountain. If your men attack those vampires outright, even with cannons, or tanks, your brave men will lose, and all will be killed, plain and simple. Those men need the element of surprise to get the upper hand and us inside to distract Fabian, and open that big door from inside. We need the vampires concentrating on Damon and me. That way we all have a chance of coming out of this alive, and of freeing the world of this contamination."

Nolan slumped in his chair. "Maybe, but you're right, I don't have a better plan, beyond nuking the place, and I'm not certain that would work, even if we could get the U.S. government to agree. Still, I'm fearful the vampires would survive. So, give us the details of your plan, please. What do we do to get by those guards outside the door, and how do we destroy the vampires once inside? Are we still using wooden stakes…and you, of course?"

Gabby leaned forward. "Okay, your troops showed that these fiends could be destroyed with stakes and with their determination…"

Nolan snickered. "And only with your Zompire help, of course. You do realize that we would have failed, if you hadn't showed up at the time you did. They had several of our men pinned down, ready for the kill. You two prevented that." He shook his head. "You won the battle, not us, not our element of surprise, or that narrow door. We needed you to finish the vampires off."

"Of course, but you may not be able to depend on Damon and myself help to get all of us out of the predicament we're going to set up. That's the nature of this trap. Damon and I may be, shall we say, tied up, and trying to stay alive…"

Nolan shook his head. "That's what worries me. Without you two, we're nothing, or *may become* nothing."

Gabby smiled. "I'm worried too, really, but, in any case, you'll be on your own until we get free. Assuming Fabian let's us into his mountain fortress in the first place, you'll have to first attack those guards with your stakes."

Beecher interrupted. "We've brought a few crossbows, not as many as I wanted, but the new order didn't come in before we left. They're only good from a short distance, but we can use them to get those wood arrows through the guards' damned hearts. Assuming we can get within firing range, and fire them accurately." He lowered his head. "Once we get inside, they may be useless."

Damon gazed at Beecher. "That's a good plan, but you've got to be careful in approaching those guards. They have super hearing. They're likely to hear any minor noise you make, even walking on the leaves on the ground. If they give Fabian's vampires a warning, they'll attack you in the open. I'm not sure you would be successful then. If that happens, Gabby and I may be as good as dead."

CHAPTER 56

DOUBLE-DOUBLE-CROSS

Fabian glared at Smithe and Enoch in his room. He strolled around his shiny metal desk, as if he had not a care in the world, and then sat in his huge, black-leather chair. The leather screamed at his weight. His smile exuded confidence that he hadn't felt since sending Vampire DeVoie to fetch Damon for use in his experiments. Of course, Damon had put an end to that hope when he fought DeVoie, and pushed him into the bright sunlight. Fabian's follow up offer to Damon was nixed when the zombie couriers had disobeyed orders, and attacked the Zompires. But now, Damon and Gabby had presented him another chance to gain his ultimate goal, control of the Human Race through Damon's DNA, and, possibly, the formation of vampire-zombies.

"Now that Damon and Gabby have agreed to meet with me, I've got another chance to capture Damon and his Dracula-inherited-blood."

Smithe leaned forward. "Excuse me, Master Fabian, I don't mean to speak out of order, but shouldn't we suspect a double cross from those miserable Zompires."

Fabian smiled, and nodded. "Why, yes, of course, Smithe. So, I am planning a double-double cross. They are probably suspicious, and will be expecting us to do something like that anyway. So, why disappoint them?" He leaned across the desk. "Here's how we're going to get around that. First, I'll invite them in, and ask them what Zompire Gabby has in mind...what's her plan to save both sides? They'll come in without suspecting a thing, stupid as they are! I plan to pretend to attack them *after* hearing their ridiculous plan...or maybe *before*. We'll see. I say pretend, because that won't be our real attack. That we'll keep in reserve. No, they won't suspect anything."

"How does that help us?"

"Easy, once they think they are under attack, they'll launch their attack on us. We'll then launch our real attack on them, capture them, and use them any way we wish...unless our first attack defeats them outright. Then, there's no need for a second attack."

"Do you have any idea what their attack will consist of?"

Fabian squinted. "I can't be sure, but, based on the attack on our friends at the Police Station, they've armed their troops with wooden stakes. Fine, but those are close range weapons, and all those troops have to get by our guards outside first, if they want to prevent them from sounding the alarm. Those guards may have to give up their lives for our cause." He shrugged. "It can't be helped. I have already prepared for that. Once their troops are inside, our second, more decisive attack begins, if necessary. They cannot overwhelm our numbers. So, we attack them in our superior numbers. We will succeed this time without doubt."

"Yes, Master Fabian. I have no doubt of that, providing we can prevent those Zompires from helping them. That's the only reason we lost at the Police Station. Once they entered the battle, and began killing us in the air, the fight was lost. They are even faster than us. We didn't stand a chance. It was a massacre."

"Don't worry, Smithe, we'll have our revenge at this encounter. There's no way we're ever going to lose to them again. I have a foolproof plan for their destruction, and it starts almost as soon as they arrive. By the time their police attack our guards, those Zompires will be totally in my control. They're doomed. So, go tell them I'll listen to their offer open-minded, but only if the meeting occurs here, at our headquarters. Tell them I won't meet anywhere else to hear their offer. I'm sure they'll adjust their plans, expecting a double cross from us, and will feel confident they can overcome anything we throw at them. They're stupid enough to fall for that. So, let them come and attack us as we talk, if I allow the negotiations to go that far. Then, we'll spring our trap." His gaze shot to the ceiling, as he yelled, "Vampires forever!"

CHAPTER 57

GUARDS

After hearing from Smithe, Damon and Gabby flew to within one hundred yards of Fabian's hideout. They landed, and morphed to human form. They then began a long, slow meander toward the door, protected by the guards who talked casually, and were not standing at attention as they had on the Zompire's last visit.

One guard lifted a phone, hidden behind a rock, and hurried to speak into it. "They're here. Tell Fabian."

As the Zompires approached, the vampires' incisor teeth began to grow. They drooled thick, green mucus. They assumed a fighting-preparation stance, with backs bent, and hands with extended claws held before their faces. They issued a low, guttural growl.

Gabby grunted. "If that stance is supposed to scare us, it's not even close. We're here on an invitation from Fabian. I assume he told you to let us pass unharmed. Now, open the door for us before we tear you apart, and feed your hearts to those disgusting zombies Fabian keeps for pets."

Both vampires stood upright, lowered their hands, and withdrew their teeth. The one closest to the approaching Zompires spoke first. "Yeah, you're right…if that is who you are. How do we know you're those miserable Zompires?"

It was Damon's turn to grunt. "I don't know about the *miserable* part, but who else do you think would approach this so-called hideout, and ask to enter? Only Zompires, carrying Fabian's verbal invitation would be bold enough to do it. That's who! Anyone else would be terrified to approach his vampire guards. Now, quit all this fooling around, and let us in, or we'll carry out Gabby's threat."

"We don't do well with threats."

"Then consider it a warning. In any case, open those doors, and let us in, or answer to Fabian."

The vampire who had made the call retreated to the closed door, and opened a panel along its left side. He placed his hand on a glass panel, allowed the light to read his palm, and then turned the handle within to the right. As he did so, the giant rock at the entrance slid to the right, and out of sight. "That last threat is worse than the female Zompire's threat. Okay, Fabian's expecting you. Before you go complaining to Fabian about your reception out here, remember, it's our job to protect the approach to the entrance to our nest. We were only acting as if an intruder had approached."

Gabby nodded. "Noted! We're here to talk to Fabian. You guards are *nothing* in our eyes. Go back to your guarding business while we converse inside. Now, get out of our way."

The vampires stood on either side of the doorway as the Zompires passed. The vampires stared at them, and bowed, laughing at them under their breaths as they passed.

"Zompire assholes," one stated just above a whisper. "I hope Fabian kills them as soon as they get inside."

"No chance," the other replied as he turned the handle to close the door. "He needs them alive for a little while." He held up one thin, crooked finger. "Then, he'll kill them…taking his time and with a great deal of pain, I hope."

The two chuckled as the stone door slid closed.

Damon sneered, and gazed at Gabby. "I told you he'd double cross us. I'm still not sure this is a good idea."

Gabby smiled. "Into the fire…"

Damon looked Heavenward. "Right!"

CHAPTER 58

ARRIVAL

Gabby and Damon shot their gazes around the enormous cave. Along the top of a ramp surrounding the cave stood multiple vampires. They snarled at them, the fiends' teeth growing amid thick foul smelling saliva. Gabby and Damon raised their gaze to the top of the ramp where Fabian stood.

Fabian descended the ramp toward his guests. "Down, comrades! These are our guests. We mean them no harm. Down, All! Back to your own duties and rooms. Damon and Gabby, I'm Supreme Vampire Fabian. Welcome to my home…under a truce flag."

Gabby smiled, and whispered, "Right! Guests…like we believe that."

Damon spoke out of the side of his mouth. "You get down too, Gabby! We're on their side. Remember! Besides their hearing is as good as our."

Gabby hung her head. "Okay, I'll back off, but I'm not happy with that!"

Damon stared at Fabian. "Remember, you had asked for a meeting us by your machete message. That failed. So, let's give this replacement meeting a chance to succeed. We're here. There's no turning back now. Let's talk."

As the Zompires proceeded deeper into the chamber, Fabian continued his walk down the ramp. He stared at a few vampires who maintained their aggressive stances, and had not as yet moved. "Comrade Vampires, I told you to return to your duties in your rooms. Do so, now!"

All the vampires turned, and disappeared into various compartments surrounding the main chamber, and down a connecting corridor, both below the ramp and beyond the top where Fabian had emerged.

Gabby smiled. "That's encouraging." She abruptly bent at her waist, and placed her hand on her expanding abdomen. "Ouch! Our baby is unhappy. Maybe he, or she doesn't like the situation, or trust Fabian. Good baby! You have excellent discernment abilities already."

Damon placed a gentle hand on her back, and, tried to help her stand upright with the other. "Are you Okay?"

"Not sure. Our baby is stirring, and kicking.."

"Do you want to leave? You've given us a legitimate reason to cancel all this. It's not too late to turn back."

"No! We've got to meet Fabian as planned. Let's not delay. I'll be fine." She took several deep breaths.

"Okay, but if you feel ill at all, let me know, and we'll leave. The heck with Fabian…and your plan."

Gabby smiled, as she continued to massage her abdomen.

Damon frowned. "By the way, what is your due date?"

"Don't know for sure." She shook her head, the movement almost imperceptible. "Not sure about anything. Never been pregnant before, and certainly not as a Zompire. I don't even know how long I've been pregnant."

"Great, a bloodthirsty vampire and a pregnant wife at the same time." He shook his head. "I'm afraid dealing with either is not going to be easy."

"Sorry." She stood upright, even though the movement increased her pain. "Okay. I'm feeling better now." She continued rubbing her abdomen. "Calm, Baby! Calm down! Please! We'll be fine. I promise. We know what we're doing."

Fabian stopped near the base of the ramp. "Are you Okay? You don't look too well."

"I'm fine, or will be soon. I hope! I'm pregnant. Baby is stirring. That's all."

"Hey! Congratulations. The first Zompire baby! You must be so proud."

"Yes, but that's a secondary issue right now. My baby is secondary. Our meeting is much more important. Let's get it on."

"Okay. You're choice!" A red light on the wall, lit by the outside guards, indicated they sensed the police approaching. With the speed of lightning,

Fabian jumped into an adjacent door, and slammed the metal door closed behind him. "Now! Spring the trap!"

CHAPTER 59

THE TRAP

Both Zompires assumed a ready stance, their arms stretched in front of their faces, their knees bent, ready for a fight. From above, the metal-on-metal sound of chains unwinding blasted in their ears. They looked up, ready to jump out of the way of any danger. Neither moved, however, frozen as they watched a large net drop toward them from the ceiling, some thirty feet above.

Damon said, "A net? Really? That won't even slow us down."

Gabby raised her hands above her head, ready to catch the net, and fling it away. "Do you think we are fish you can catch with ease, Fabian? I'd jump out of the way, but instead, I think I'll cast the net in your direction. You'd better be prepared to be caught in your own vampire net!"

Fabian watched on a video screen with image focused on the Zompires. He belly laughed as the nets journeyed toward the Zompires. His gaze followed the nets as if he was in the chamber with the Zompires.

The nets hit the Zompires hard as if they were fully loaded tractor-trailer trucks, not nets. Both bent at the knees, and were further dragged to the ground before they could either toss the net aside, or jump from under it. Both felt weakness descend through their body from head to feet. They became nauseated and helpless beneath the metal and rubber that made up the net.

Worried about the baby growing inside her, Gabby twisted as the net crushed her to the ground. She landed on her side, thinking that way the net would not crush her swollen abdomen and her baby. She found she couldn't move, couldn't even lift the net even a few inches. She had thought it would be so easy to discard, and throw it at Fabian. She would have liked to catch him in the precarious situation she found herself in now. The pungent smell of garlic wafted into her nose, paralyzing her. She found she could move only her head, and that only slowly. She looked toward Damon, who also remained frozen beneath the net pinning him to the ground. "What the Heck, Damon?"

Damon stared at his love. "I can't move a muscle, Gabby. How about you?"

"The same. We should be able to toss these nets as if they were made of paper. I wish we could have, and put Fabian in this crushing predicament instead of us. I don't understand."

Fabian emerged from the room he had ducked into with a huge smile. "Confused, My Dear

225

Zompires?" He strolled down the rest of the ramp toward them. "Let me explain. You're right, Gabby...I can call you Gabby, can't I?"

Gabby began having some difficulty breathing because of the weight crushing her. She worried about her baby. She had to keep breathing, and stop fighting against the net's weight to ensure enough oxygen got to her baby. She growled. "You can call me anything you want, but when I get out from under here, I'm going to tear that stone heart of yours out of your chest, and crush it into non-existence. I'll rip open your skull to get at your miniscule brain, which I think I'll then feed to your zombies. It'll probably make them ill, however."

"Wow! You *are* really mad at me, but you may regret those biting words, and sooner than you think."

"I doubt that. Those words are all true. You can count on it. I figure we will be freed from here within a few minutes. You'd better prepare for my onslaught very soon, Oh, Fabian Vampire With No Feelings."

Fabian shook his head. "Oh, I'm sure all your threats are true, as far as you think they are. I'm sure you mean every word. Remember who is captured and who is free and in charge." He lost the smile, and frowned. "And I mean every word I say to you and Damon, and I'm afraid that's not so good for you."

Gabby shook her head again. "When I get out of this temporary, and I do mean *temporary*, jail, I'm going to enjoy destroying you. Believe me!"

226

CHAPTER 60

THREATS

While Gabby kept Fabian busy with threats, Damon tried unsuccessfully to raise his head. He finally gave up, and raised his voice, "Threats aside, Fabian, I thought this was supposed to be a peaceful meeting. We didn't suspect any double cross."

"Peaceful? Double cross?" Fabian placed his hand over his heart. "I don't know where you got that idea. After all, you set up the meeting, not me. When I sent one of my vampires to meet you at your home with an entourage of zombies to try to get you here peacefully, you destroyed every zombie, every single one! I'm glad I had the foresight to record a message in that machete. Those poor zombies never stood a chance with you two."

Gabby laughed. "Two? I destroyed them *all by myself.* I didn't need any help from Damon."

Fabian held up one finger, as if signaling a waiter. "Exactly my point. Instead of finding out why they were there, you used your superior powers to destroy them. And now you expect me to trust you to come into my hideout under a flag of truce, and not attack my

vampires, zombies and me?" He squinted his eyes.
"What about those policemen approaching outside?
Are they here for our *peaceful* meeting? I sincerely
doubt it. I'd have to be crazy to assume that."

Gabby snorted. "Now, *crazy* I'd agree with. If
you suspected we had something foul in mind, why let
us in at all? Why not simply repel us as we forced our
way in?"

He shook his head, and placed his hands in front
of him, as if repelling the Zompires. "Oh, I respect
your powers. You've demonstrated superior strength,
speed and so forth by destroying my original
representative, Vampire DeVoie along with his
zombies. Then you did the same to the same those
zombies I sent to your home, and you did it with the
ease of a flyswatter against an old fly. You then
destroyed my vampires at the Police Station who were
keeping the human policemen in check." He pointed
toward the main door to the chamber. "That red light
blinking over there means those same human survivors
are trying to get in right now." He shook his head. "I
don't want to challenge your powers. No way! I either
need Damon on my side, or a large sample of his blood
to use for research. Either will do. So, I thought I
could accomplish both by agreeing to this meeting, and
then trapping you inside my hideout in my Double-
Double-Cross, as I have now." You should have
forgotten your Double Cross, and have *really* intended
to have a peaceful discussion with me with no police

force behind you." He took a deep breath before speaking. "However, I learned a lot about you Zompires. I knew you would be deceitful, and would try to destroy us, not make us a *so-called peaceful offer.* I decided a Double-Double-Cross was called for to get you two in here incapacitated by my magic nets and your backup troops stuck outside our impenetrable door. I won't apologize for my actions, nor do I regret my decision."

Damon frowned, again trying to lift his cover. He failed. He couldn't even get his shoulder off the ground. He felt his Zompire strength draining from his normally strong body. "Why can't we move this net? It must weight ten thousand pounds, but I still should be able to budge it a little."

Fabian shook his head. "No, no. It's not the weight that's holding you down. It's something much more sinister. I really thought you'd have figured it out by now. It's Garlic. Don't you smell it?"

CHAPTER 61

GARLIC

Damon continued to struggle against the net. It refused to move. "Garlic?"

"Exactly!"

"What's that got to do with all this?"

Garlic is one of all vampires' greatest nemeses. Smithe informed me that you avoided coming close to the garlic the police had hung above the door." He paced back and forth with his hands clenched behind his back. "It gave me pause to think. I thought that maybe garlic might be one of your weaknesses also." He spun toward his captives, and shrugged. "I had no way of testing that theory, since I know of no Zompires except you two. I experimented on a few of my vampire underlings. If they came within a few inches, they disintegrated as if they had been stabbed through the heart." He placed a bent finger under his chin. "Lost several vampires doing that. Unfortunate, but necessary."

With a mighty exertion, Damon shook his head. The effort gave him a splitting headache. "You're sick, Fabian."

"Maybe! Anyway, I wondered about my zombies. They were unaffected by garlic."

Damon's gaze shot around the net. "I don't see the garlic, but I can smell it. Where is it?"

Fabian laughed. "I thought you'd never ask! *Distance* is the answer. I had my zombies rub garlic on every surface of those nets. We found that if heavily coated with garlic, none of my vampires could get within 20 feet of the net without being repelled. I found that a lighter application allows even me to stand within 2 feet of the garlic-coated nets."

Gabby snorted. "Let me guess. You had your vampires test the distances, right? That's how you lost them."

Fabian bowed. "But of course. Why would I risk myself? I'm too important to risk injury. We weren't sure of the amount that would be effective against you. However, I hoped that, since the surface area is so large, smaller amounts of garlic would be effective. I guess I was right again."

"Your vampires risked their lives to find that out?"

"Right you are, Zompire Gabby! I'm surprised you show concern for my vampires."

Gabby closed her eyes, and shook her head. The effort gave her a headache also. "I wasn't at all concerned about your fiends…only the disgusting fact you were willing to risk them, even if only to repel them. They mean nothing to you! Do they?"

"Nope! None! Now, your loving husband is different. He's *very* dear to me. So, don't worry. I'll free him to collect his blood if he shows any signs of deterioration. I reasoned correctly, that those bodies of yours would act like the half vampires you are. I had hoped that the zombie part of you would not prevail in your reaction to the garlic. Brilliant, right?"

Damon tried to lift the chain, again to no avail. "Brilliant? Ha! Suppose the garlic had disintegrated our bodies like your vampires? Then, you'd have none of my blood to make your vaccine with. Not so brilliant!"

"That was a chance I had to take. I reasoned that you Zompires are so powerful that your bodies would fight it off for a while anyway, but don't worry, I'm not going to wait too long to harvest your blood, Damon. Not to worry! That will be soon, long before you disintegrate." He shook his head, and frowned. "You should have agreed to join us with my initial machete invitation."

Gabby fought to raise her head, accomplishing only an inch. "Go to Hell!"

"Probably. I also thought of using a giant Cross, but that would also affect us."

Damon laughed. The effort strained his chest muscles, making them ache, as if he had been coughing for weeks. "We Zompires aren't affected by any Cross. We love it, and what it stands for."

"Yes, I had heard that also. I wasn't sure it was true, but that was the second reason you now see no Cross in front of you. Showing you a Cross would have been my backup plan. If the garlic failed, my zombies would bring out several Crosses to corral you, and you would have never seen me. I would have stayed in my room. After all, I couldn't risk you running amok at my dwelling place, now, could I?"

"That's because you're afraid of us. Besides, you desperately need to use his blood, specifically his DNA, for your own evil purposes."

"Granted! I tried to get him, well both of you, to come here by sending my original invitation via zombies. When that failed, I thought of ways I could get you here…how to get you, err…him, here, so I can get his all-important, inherited Count Dracula DNA. I need him either totally cooperative, which I now realize is impossible, or at least under my power, my spell, so to speak, as you both are right now. If you noticed, I jumped into that room when the net fell, just in case the garlic, like the Cross, didn't also affect you. I now see that extra precaution was unnecessary."

Through her increasing weakness, Gabby spoke, "So, what happens now? Do you harvest his DNA, and then dispose of us, now that you know we're never going to join you of our own free will?"

Fabian approached the two while pulling a machete from its sheath at his side. "Not exactly! You see, My Dear Female Zompire…" he looked upward..."I need Damon for a while longer, but you, I'm not so sure. I noticed you were expecting a baby any day now...big bulge and all that...I'm right about your due date too, am I not?"

"Yeah, so what?"

"Well, I don't need you at all, and I certainly don't need you producing more Zompires whom I probably cannot control either. So, you, My Dear, are expendable, always have been, and now you'll meet that God you're always praying to. Hope God is waiting for you."

Fabian approached Gabby with his gaze fixed on her neck while raising the machete overhead."

CHAPTER 62

DEATH

As Fabian approached Gabby with a humongous smile on his face, Gabby struggled to free herself from the heavy burden on her. She only managed to force her head, neck and upper chest a few inches from its weight.

Fabian donned a concerned look. "What's the matter dear? Can't free yourself?" He gazed at the ceiling. "Of course, that's the whole idea." His gaze returned to the struggling Gabby. "But don't struggle too much. You see, I'm about to free you of this burden."

"When I get free of this *burden*, as you call it, I'm going to burden your life with its end, and believe me you won't like it. I promise you that I'll crush you and all your followers."

Fabian shook his head. "Oh, what a terrible thought. Well, I'm not worried about any of your hollow threats. You see, I have no intention of letting you, or Damon get free of my garlic net trap."

Gabby sneered. "I think you'll be surprised at the strength and versatility of we Zompires. We'll free ourselves from your garlic nets soon, and then, you've had it."

Fabian bowed. "Believe me, I acknowledge your Zompires' strength and abilities. That's why I've prepared for your visit."

Damon gave up trying to lift the net. "OK, Fabian. Enough talk. You and Gabby can joust later. All your threats mean nothing to us. We came here to make you an offer. Instead, we find ourselves double-crossed, and having threats hurled at us with every breath. Enough is enough! Free us, and let us explain our offer to you. You're a fool if you don't"

Fabian's hand shot to his chest. "A fool? Is that what you think of me. I can understand Gabby's contempt for me. She thinks she's superior to vampires, to me, but, no, she finds herself subdued, and under my control." He shook his head again. "No, not a fool, but a very careful vampire who has achieved something no one else ever has, the conquest of the infamous Zompires. By the way, I figured you would come with backup. I assume they're trying to get in as we speak." He shook his head. "They won't succeed. The door is locked from the inside, and can only be opened by pressing that green button against the wall. It's a safety locking mechanism I had installed against crowds with wooden stakes trying to get in,. Now, I find it very useful against your backup. Ha, ha, ha, ha."

Gabby struggled to get her shoulders from under the net. Succeeding, she now found the net folded over onto itself, crushing her beneath it. She gazed at the green button, aglow from within. "So, now what Fabian?"

Fabian smiled, and held his hands out to the sides, the machete dangling from his fingers. "Now, we find out something else about you Zompires that I've wondered since your formation."

Gabby shook her head, trying to clear her foggy mind from the effects of the garlic. "And what's that, Fabian?"

Fabian ran the last few yards, getting to Gabby's side as Gabby struggled to free her hands. "To find out if beheading a Zompire will kill it, or not."

Damon screamed, "No!"

Fabian laughed as he raised the machete above his head and brought it down with all the strength he could muster. The machete met Gabby's neck, exposed above the net. The sharp blade sliced through her neck, severing her head from her body. The head rolled 2 feet away, landing on its right side, her non-seeing eyes fixed open, staring at Fabian and his blood-soaked machete. Her body flopped once, and then did not move.

CHAPTER 63

POLICE BACKUP

As dawn arrived, Nolan and Beecher drove to the cave area with their caravan of police, Beecher said, "Are we sure Damon's plan for us to take out any guards will work?"

Nolan, who was driving, glanced at Beecher. "I'm not worried about that. It's daytime. No self-respecting vampire should be outside now anyway. Even if they're in some cave in the mountain, I've never known vampires to use tactical weapons like guns. They depend on fear, terror and those devastating teeth to attack…at night."

"So who do you think will be guarding the place?"

"I suspect their zombies. That's why I gave the order to shot for their heads and hearts at the same time, but there may be no guards posted at all. Who knows how these vampires think? I told them to use the cross bows with wooden shafts to be sure. Remember, this Fabian doesn't know we're coming as back up. I'm sure for all the time that they've been hiding in there, they've never planned on an assault like we're bringing." He thumbed toward the caravan behind him. "Even if he suspects we're coming, he doesn't have to post any guards. He can simply lock the door to the mountain. He thinks we have no way of getting in. He doesn't know that the Zompires are planning to double-cross him, and plan to open the door from inside…we hope!"

"Sounds good, but sounds like it could have a whole bunch of disasters built in. What if Fabian double-crosses Damon? What if the door has a special code to open? How is Damon going to get the code to open it? Suppose Fabian kills Damon and Gabby somehow? Then what?"

Nolan frowned, and again glanced at Beecher. His gaze returned slowly to the road before them. "Then, we wait for nightfall, and attack them as they emerge. With any luck, they'll send the guards out first, and we can destroy them." He shrugged. "Hopefully, we'll destroy them while the door is open so we can rush in, and destroy all of them."

"And if the vampire guards close the door before we destroy them?"

"Then we hope we can figure our how to open the door. Maybe they'll use the closing mechanism outside. We can use the same mechanism to open the door, and help our friends inside."

Beecher frowned. "Doesn't sound so easy to me."

"Yeah, I agree. It sounded a whole lot easier when Damon and Gabby presented this attack plan to us."

Beecher leaned his head back against the headrest. "Do you think we stand any chance to destroy *every one* of the fiends in there? I mean, they're awfully powerful. If even one gets away, that one will spread their vampirism, kind of like they have already." He shook his head. This is sounding more and more like an insurmountable task that we've gotten ourselves into."

Nolan nodded, and frowned deeper. "Yes, it does sound that way, doesn't it? But what you suggest is the worse case scenario. It doesn't take into account our Zompire friends. They're an amazing duo, a duo with tremendous power, even more than those vampires. What I don't know is if it'll be enough against this vampire clan. We don't know how many vampires are in there. We can only hope we can overcome them, keep our losses to a minimum, and succeed…for all Mankind's sake."

"Amen to that! Amen to that!"

CHAPTER 64

BIRTH

Fabian continued to laugh as he watched Gabby's severed head. "Look at that! She's smiling! I do believe she enjoyed having me do that. I thought the Zompire female to be an airhead. Guess I was right." He smiled, and walked over to it. He kicked it toward her torso. It stopped a foot from Gabby, facing her body. Her eyes were open, as if staring at the rest of her, or staring into infinity, but seeing nothing. Blood oozed from her mouth, and found its way down her cheek, dripping onto the ground, drop by drop. Her body jerked erratically, and then stopped all movement.

Damon screamed at the horrible site. "No! Gabby, No!" A flood of tears began streaming down his cheek. He reared up, again trying to lift the net with no success. "What have you done, Fabian? How can you expect me to meet your demand to work with you after you…killed my beloved Gabby?" He screamed, as he had never done before. "I'll never cooperate with you now, You Selfish, Unfeeling Fiend."

Fabian laughed, and then smiled. He extended his arms before him. "I don't need your cooperation,

Damon. I knew from the time you destroyed Vampire DeVoie that your cooperation was a pipe dream. He was my emissary, an emissary of hope for all vampires and for you, but you destroyed that hope before even giving him a chance. You destroyed, not only him, but all his zombies too. They had been sent there to serve him…and you."

"Serve me? First, DeVoie bit me. Then The zombies tried to eat me. That's how I got turned into this Zompire, instead of simply a vampire. I guess both bites together were stronger than DeVoie's single bite. Those zombies ruined your plans forever."

Fabian began a slow walk in Damon's direction. "Yes, that was regrettable, I'm afraid. DeVoie had made those beings as a new type of zombie-slave to serve him and me. I permitted it because I thought they might be useful to us, and with the slight intelligence they had retained, they might serve me…and you even better. Instead, you and Gabby destroyed them all. Then, you went on to destroy *my* zombies I sent to your home with my invitation."

"They attacked us."

"Again regrettable. They overstepped their authority. They deserved what they got, I guess."

"You guess? You vampire fiend!" The tears began to gush from his eyes. He pressed harder against the floor to no effect. The net refused to yield. He yelled, "I hate you, Fabian! Gabby didn't deserved what you did to her! We came here under a flag of truce to present an idea of Gabby's, not mine! You then attack us, behead Gabby, and then say all that has happened is *regrettable* in your eyes? You'll regret not hearing her idea. It was beneficial to the vampires, the Human Race and we Zompires. It may have even saved you. Now, you have no chance of surviving our intervention here, and you're going to take all your vampires and zombies with you to everlasting Hell."

Fabian thumbed his nose. "I don't give a rat's ass about the Human Race, you two, or Gabby's stupid idea. You must think I'm stupid." He shook his head, his gaze fixed on Damon, wishing he could melt him with his gaze. "I knew from the start what that offer was, a way to get in here for both you and, after you open those doors for your human friends waiting outside. I won't let that confrontation take place, My Dear Damon." He closed his eyes, and shook his head. "Not that I have any doubt about how that confrontation would end. We would easily destroy all of you, like I destroyed that damnable Zompire." He pointed to Gabby without taking his gaze from Damon. "I've outsmarted you, My Dear Zompire, Damon."

Between sobs, Damon screamed, "You're overconfident!"

"I doubt that. I've gone out of my way to offer you peace, to get you to join us. If, as I first proposed through DeVoie, you had joined us, we both would have had an unlimited supply of human blood for food, your dear Gabby would still be alive, and the Human

Race would be content, giving us blood, as they do for their pitiful blood banks for their use..." He paused with outstretched arms... "same idea, with only we Vampires and Zompires benefiting, not the Human Race you seem to care about so much.

"I'm still going to tear your heart out, and feed it to your zombies. Gabby might not be able to keep her promise to destroy you, but *I will!*"

Fabian laughed. "You'll never get the chance. Can't you see the position you're in? You're in my power. I can take all the blood I need from your body now. I have a zombie who used to be a physician. She's good at blood drawing. So, you can forget any attempt at revenge." He tilted his head. "Sorry."

"I'll bet."

Suddenly, Gabby's body jerked, her back arching for a full minute. The net rose a few inches. Her body settled onto the floor. It stopped moving. From between her legs, slithered a four-foot long, four-inch wide, speckled snake, hissing as it crawled from beneath the net. It began to grow, and to grow to over twenty feet long and two feet wide.

Fabian screamed, "What the..."

CHAPTER 65

SNAKE

The snake slithered in circles around Gabby, licking her severed head with its forked tongue, and then, after a few seconds, headed for Damon. The snake stopped at Damon's head, then licked several of the tears, streaming down his face. It then turned back to Gabby's head, slithering as fast as it could, its tail whacking Damon's cheek in passing. It then encircled her head, squeezing it, causing an increase in the exsanguination from Gabby's neck.

Slithering toward Gabby's body, the snake never released the head, instead dragging it toward her body. After its head reached the still body of its mother, the snake licked both the neck and the blood. Satisfied these two items were the same, it contorted its body, placing the head in the correct position, facing to the side, upon Gabby's body.

Fabian frowned, "Where did that thing come from? I knew you Zompires were snakes-in-the-grass mutants, but a real snake from a dead Zompire is beyond belief." He shook his head. "Wait a minute! Could it be?" He laughed, and then pointed at the snake, currently encircling Gabby's head and neck as it forced its way under her. "Look at that, Damon. The dumb snake thinks it can reattach Gabby's head to her body. Foolish snake!" He shook his head. "You and Gabby were foolish, thinking you could come in here to attack us. Simply foolish!"

Damon stopped crying, and continued to stare at the snake's movement, as it twirled its body around Gabby's head and shoulders.

Fabian drew a little closer to the spectacle. "Oh, how sweet! It's hugging its mother." His gaze fell upon Damon as he said, "Did you know your wife would give birth to a snake, a reptile, destined to crawl on its stomach all its life, like the Devil in the Garden of Eden?" He shook his head again. "You Zompires are full of surprises."

Damon lifted his head, but still could not budge the net. "You'd be surprised."

"Oh, I am already. Imagine, a snake-in the-grass from another snake-in-the-grass. Who would have thought?" He strolled over to Damon. "That's why I needed you to volunteer your blood, your DNA, to our cause. You and your recently departed wife could have joined us as we imprisoned all human society to be under our control. Instead, you've become entrapped by the superior intelligence of your vampire enemies, specifically *my* intelligence. How does that make you feel…inferior, I hope, because you are!" He laughed as he doubled over with mirth.

Damon growled. "Let me out from under this net, and I'll show you who's inferior, You Vampire Fiend Murderer!"

"You've resorted to name calling. I'm not surprised. You have no other choice. You are powerless to do anything else." He put his hands on his hips. "Now, we need to discuss that DNA I mentioned. I'll give you one more chance to join forces with me. I shouldn't, but I decided I will." He took a deep breath. "You've already lost your wife and...whatever you call that snake-baby. By the way is it a son, or a daughter?" He shook his head. "No matter, whatever it is, if you join us, I'll let it live. If not, I'll find a way to destroy it. I could always get a mongoose to eat it." He placed a finger under his chin. "Wait a minute. If that's your offspring, presumably, it should have your DNA. I'll have to check that before trying to destroy it. I may not need you after all. All I have to do is put that thing in a tank of some type. Actually, it doesn't matter if that snake's DNA works, or not, now that I think of it. I'll still take some of your blood." He paused for a few seconds. "I think I'll take *all* of your blood." He bowed his head slightly. "Sorry...well, no I'm not, really. Anyway, that should help our vampire scientists make the DNA soup...that's what I call it...that they will use to experiment on your ancestor's original DNA. That DNA is what makes you so supreme. Right? Of course it is! That's why you are so powerful." He paused, and smiled wryly. "So, our scientists will use that soup to immunize the human race against the virus, or whatever it is that causes vampirism. That way, the humans will be immune to vampire bites." He smiled. "They'll be willing donors once they learn they and their offspring will never become vampires. They will never die from a vampire bite. Never! It's brilliant! Don't you agree?"

Damon growled. "No! The humans will destroy you anyway. They won't give you fiends anything, especially their blood."

Damon turned his gaze upon the snake-Gabby combination. As he watched, tendrils of sinews began to grow from her neck to the head and vice-versa. The tendrils pulled the head toward the body until they met. Damon's mouth opened wide.

Observing Damon's gaze, Fabian also turned his gaze toward Gabby. "What the Hell? What's going on? Is that snake really trying to reattach Gabby's head to her body? That's impossible! The dumb snake! I guess it takes after its mother and father. It's downright dumb! You tried to do the impossible, destroy all the vampires. The humans will also fail, if they ever do try, as you suggested." He shook his head again, slower this time. "Now, your dumb child is trying to attach a severed head. None of what it's trying to do is going to work. That dumb animal doesn't even know when to quit. It'll need an awful lot of glue and a lot of luck to accomplish what it's trying to do."

CHAPTER 66

REBIRTH

The snake completely encircled Gabby's head and neck. Neither Damon, nor Fabian, could see what the snake had accomplished within its coils. The snake hugged her mother's head tighter, and tighter.

Fabian tilted his head. "Oh, look at that! The snake is hugging her. How sweet. It's going to be disappointed, though, when its mother doesn't respond." He snapped his head upright. "Besides, even if Gabby could try hugging her offspring-snake, she couldn't because of the net forcing her down. As soon as that stupid snake realizes what it's trying to do is futile, I'll capture it for my use." He turned his gaze to Damon. "See, I can be sensitive to other's wants and desires. I'm allowing the snake a few moments to try to get her to respond, and not killing it outright. Then, I'll capture, and enslave it. You Zompires claim to be more human than we vampires. You claim to still believe in, and love God. We don't, but we can still feel compassion to another creature. Don't you agree? Aren't I showing a good example of vampire compassion?"

Damon lifted his head a few inches. "Bullshit! You're only waiting as you try to figure out how to catch a huge snake, something you have no experience in doing. It has nothing to do with compassion. If you had true compassion, you would have let us discuss our offer to you, not trapped us, killed Gabby, and then tormented me by threatening my offspring."

"True, I guess, but I'm also curious what's going to happen next. Assuming I'm right, and Gabby won't miraculously resurrect, I'd like to see how the snake reacts to its failure. But you're wrong overall. I have some experiences with large snakes from a visit to Africa years back…not any this large obviously, but that snake poses no danger to me. If it tried to attack me, I'd simply change into a bat and fly away, or a giant wolf, and kill it." He walked closer to the snake. "Besides, killing it wood be so easy without morphing. A burst from a fire extinguisher, which one of my vampires, a previous firefighter, brought with him, and the snake will freeze, and be unable to move. Then, if I wanted it dead, like its mother, I would simply chop off its head. I'd burn the carcass before it got a chance to regenerate, in case it's one of those animals that can do that. We vampires, as you know, have no use for a fire. We're terrified of it because it would destroy us. That same firefighter-vampire I mentioned brought matches and gas for fuel. Don't know why, nor do I care. If I didn't need it for DNA experimentation, your offspring could be destined for a bonfire. However, do not fear, its destined for my scientific vampire lab."

Damon growled loudly once more, but refused to converse further with Fabian.

Suddenly, Gabby's body jerked three times. The snake released its grip on her head and upper body, and uncoiled to reveal Gabby's head neatly attached to its neck.

"Woo! Will you look at that! The snake actually reattached her head. Glad she still is covered by the net! Guess I'd better kill that meddling snake right away before it does something else undesirable. I guess the show is over." He cupped his hands around his mouth, and yelled, "Hey, Lynch, get me that fire extinguisher and the fire making material Zeke brought. I think it's going to come in *very* handy. I need it...now!"

The snake curled itself on the floor beside Gabby, looking very much like a cobra, about to be hypnotized by a snake charmer. Instead, it extended its body far above the floor, and morphed into a twelve-foot high grey wolf, with drool dripping from its mouth. It growled loudly, filling the chamber with its vicious sound. Its retracted lips exposed its six-inch long incisors.

Lynch froze when he entered the chamber. "What the Hell is that, and where did it come from?"

Fabian retreated up the ramp to where Lynch stood. "Never mind that! Give me those things." He threw the fire extinguisher at the wolf, which knocked it to one side, using a flick of its jaw. "I guess we'll have to set fire to it." He lit the stick with the matches.

The wolf ignored Fabian and Lynch, and bent down, gripping the net with its teeth. It shook its head to the side, and the net flew to the wall of the cave.

Fabian's eyes flew open. "Better get every one out here now. We have an uninvited guest, an intruder that we have to destroy. Kill it!"

Gabby suddenly sat up. "Leave my daughter alone, Fabian. Your pitiful attempt to kill her with that small fire will do nothing but incite her...and me!"

Fabian threw down the flaming sticks, and yelled, "Everyone get out here, change into bats and wolves. Attack the intruders and destroy them. He then jumped into the air, converting to a six-foot bat, as the other vampires joined him.

CHAPTER 67

INFANT

Gabby leapt to her feet, and looked toward Damon as Fabian flew toward them. She pointed to Damon. "Free Damon, Girl." She shook her head. "We've got to give you a name soon. Can't keep calling you, *Girl.*"

The wolf charged toward Damon. As she had with the net covering her mother, she tossed her father's covering net aside, bouncing it off the adjacent wall as if it were a mere rag.

Gabby yelled, "Open the door, Girl!"

The wolf hesitated only for a moment, and then headed toward the door to the chamber.

Fabian morphed into a human three feet in front of Gabby. "Tell your daughter that that door is locked. It's impenetrable. She can't force it open."

With his strength returning at the speed of lightning, Damon jumped to his feet as Gabby had done. "She doesn't have to force them." He turned toward the door, and pointed to two eight-inch buttons to the right of the door. "Daughter, push the Green button. That should open the door." He then mumbled,

"I hope she knows her colors." He quickly added, "Push the one on the bottom."

Fabian laughed. "That daughter of yours was just born. She'll never understand you, not that it matters. Even if she does manage to open the door, we'll still destroy your *would be saviors*, and then you two pains."

The huge wolf paused, and stared at both Damon and then Gabby. It then shifted its gaze to the two buttons. In one fluid motion, the wolf pushed the green button with its nose, and turned to face the vampire bats charging it. The wolf then leapt into the air, and morphed in an instant to a bat whose wingspan extended over twenty feet. The bat flew toward her adversaries. With its wings spread wide, she moved toward the smaller vampire bats. As the distance between the horde and herself closed, she paused, mid air, hovered, and spread her wings wide.

The vampire bats struck her wings and her underbelly, every one of them becoming unconscious by the resultant collision. They fell unmoving to the floor. The few, who were able to change direction to avoid the collision, flew to the top of the chamber, grouping at its apex.

The large bat chased them to the ceiling, the vampire bats dispersing in several directions to avoid the pursuing enemy. They flew back to their rooms at the top of the stairs, trying to escape the fate of their fellow vampire bats.

Gabby had watched the action closely. She motioned Damon to join her, and then yelled, "Here, Daughter, come here. Don't chase them. It may be a trap. Let's help our friends in taking care of this batch of vampire bats first."

The door to the chamber had opened, and the police swarmed into the room, carrying all the weapons they could carry to kill the vampires.

Fabian, who had also watched the defeat of his vampire bats, turned to escape. The large bat landed in front of him, blocking his escape. He froze, shaking with fear.

Damon and Gabby darted to Fabian. Damon grabbed him by the back of his collar, and yanked him off his feet. Damon turned to the large bat, standing on the ramp, and flapping its wings. "Good job, Daughter."

The large bat morphed once more, this time into a nineteen inch, six-pound, naked human baby girl at Gabby's feet. She began crying.

Gabby picked up the baby. "Awwww. My guess is that our daughter is hungry." She held the baby close to her face. She smiled from ear to ear. "Isn't that right, Girl?" Gabby paused, and turned to Damon. "What do we call her, Daddy?"

"I think we should name her after her mother"

"Really? Gabriella? Okay, I'll consider that, among others."

"Okay, let's go outside for some privacy so you can breast-feed her. She spent an awful lot of energy with all those conversions, and fighting. The police can take care of the fallen vampires, and track down the zombies."

As Gabby walked toward the open door, she said to Nolan, "Destroy all those vampire bats before they recover. Give us a call if you need us to help you further."

Nolan's police began stabbing every unconscious vampire bat through its heart. The bats turned into dust with each stabbing. Not a sound emerged from the dying vampire bats. When they were finished, the floor was covered by black vampire dust. The disgusting smell of old, rotting flesh filled the air.

Nolan pointed to the top of the ramp. "Up there, now! There are vampires in those rooms. We've got to destroy every one of them. Have your guns ready also. There should be a bunch of zombies with them. Remember our instructions!"

CHAPTER 68

ZOMBIES

Damon held Fabian high above his head. "Don't try changing into anything, Fabian. Remember, I'm faster than you, and, if I have to chase you, it won't go well for you." He searched the room for Nolan, or Beecher. Spotting Nolan, he yelled, "Nolan, get some men up there fast to destroy the vampires and zombies in hiding. Tell them to be careful. They're not unconscious like those were. Tell them to enter each room with a few police as we discussed earlier. Better have those stakes and guns ready for anything."

Nolan nodded. "Already ordered." He then led a group of the police up the ramp, weapons at the ready.

Damon stared at Fabian. "Now, what do I do with you? You were so sure you had us where you wanted us, rather than the other way around. You showed no mercy in beheading Gabby." He smiled. "Besides being pregnant, did you forget she is also part zombie. I guess that helped put her back together."

Nolan and Beecher stopped at the top of the ramp. The SWAT team rushed past them, anxious for a fight.

Nolan yelled to them, "Don't go into any rooms until we're there. The doors are probably locked. So, use the battering rams we brought to smash down the door. Don't bother trying the handle."

The SWAT team members split into groups of four, and stood outside every wooden door down the hallway. Those without battering rams positioned two burly men a few feet away from their target door, ready to use their shoulders and their weight to smash the door down.

Nolan and Beecher stopped at the first door. They checked that every door was covered by SWAT before entering. Nolan gave a hand signal, first raising his arm, and then dropping his hand to his side, as if starting a race. All the battering rams smashed through the doors with a loud *crash*. The doors attacked by the shoulders also caved in.

Upon entering the first room, a vampire jumped at Nolan, gripping him by the shoulders, and forcing him to the floor. Beecher didn't hesitate, but instead thrust his stake into the vampire's back, careful not to go too far in, so as not tot puncture Nolan.

"I'm getting good at stabbing vampires without hitting the victim beneath. I sincerely hope it's a technique I never have to use again.

Nolan rolled over, shaking the vampire dust from his chest. "Disgusting! Hate the smell!" He looked to Beecher, standing above him. "Thanks, Partner."

"You're welcome. Hope you do the same for me someday...like today."

Nolan smiled, "Guaranteed! Now, let's move on to help the others." He climbed to his feet with the help of Beecher, and both rushed back into the hallway.

They were met by growling zombies, most dragging one leg behind them. All were saying, "Brains, brains, good tasting brains. Eat brains."

Beecher yelled to two SWAT team members, "Remember, aim for their heads. Destroying their brains kills them."

Nolan pulled out his revolver. "I don't think you have to remind them. We told them that already." He shot the closest zombie in the forehead, and it fell forward, unmoving. Where did they come from, anyway? I thought we had all the doorways covered."

Other zombies tripped over their fallen comrade, and began crawling toward Nolan and Beecher. "Brains. Must eat brains."

Beecher turned to the SWAT team members, coming out of the first room. "Shoot them while they're down. Remember, they're already dead. Don't hesitate." He then shot the one at his feet. He turned to Nolan. "There must have been a large meeting room somewhere at the end of this hallway that housed them. We'll check later. For now, let's kill all these." He turned to the other police. "Shoot as many as you can *in the head.*

Nolan laughed. "Again, no need for a *zombie killing lecture*! They know!"

The ensemble shot all the zombies in the hallway and added any coming up the hallway. One, or two vampires hid behind the zombie horde until they were close enough to attack. Those at the front were stabbed multiple times by the other SWAT team members. All were afraid that they would miss killing the fiends because of their mighty speed, strength, and agility. Missing the heart by only an inch could mean the difference in destroying the fiend, and become one of the undead. A few vampires flew from the rooms as tiny bats to avoid the entering police. They tried to fly close to the ceiling, out of the reach of the stakes. They succeeded.

Nolan yelled toward the ramp. "Hey, Drakes, you've got incoming vampire bats. Get them!"

Gabby quickly handed the baby to Damon, making sure he held her in his free hand and away from Fabian, who thrashed like a fish on a hook. "Hold our daughter. I've got this. I'll be right back." She gazed at the top of the ramp, and yelled to Nolan, "No problem!" She morphed into the large Eagle again. She flew to the top of the ramp, and awaited the vampire bats.

As several emerged from the hallway, they were met by the Gabby-Eagle that opened its beak, and devoured each and every one of them. When no more bats emerged, she flew near to Damon, and morphed back to her Zompire-Human form. She grabbed the baby from Damon.

Damon frowned. "Really? You ate them? They must taste terrible.'

"I wouldn't recommend them for a regular diet, but it was all I could think of to stop all of them before any of them escaped. You are right, though, they both smell and taste *lousy*."

Damon shook his head. "Better you than me. I guess this pregnancy has changed you a great deal. Hasn't it?"

"For the better, Mr. Damon Drake, for the better!"

CHAPTER 69

VAMPIRE BACK UP

Damon turned his attention to Fabian, now flapping in his hand like a child trying to escape his parents. "As I was saying, what am I to do about you?"

Fabian snarled, "It doesn't matter much. Your destiny is sealed, Oh, Formerly Great Zompire."

"Formerly Great? I think not. Remember, you're the one being suspended in the air, and don't even think about changing into some other animal, or a cloud, or anything else. I was serious. I'm ready for that, and if you try the 'I can become smoke trick' I will do the same and maintain my hold on you. You're the one whose goose is cooked, not me."

"That's what you think! Before you came, I suspected you would pull some kind of double cross, so, I sent word for every vampire in the world to appear here to help me defeat you. You see, I anticipated that you might be able to defeat our small number of vampires. Of course, I didn't see a giant snake and wolf Zompire daughter as part of that defeat…anyway, there's no way your puny army of human police and two Zompires with their bastard child could possibly defeat thousands of vampires, merging here all at once." He looked to the East. There was no sign yet of the bright sunlight of morning. "They should be arriving very soon from the east as they race here ahead of the sun. I timed it perfectly, it seems."

"Bastard child? Timed it perfectly? I sincerely doubt that, You Unholy Monster." Damon ran the few steps toward the entranceway. He carried Fabian who felt light as a feather toward Gabby, now feeding their baby.

"This Unholy Monster called our little baby a Bastard child."

Gabby stared at Fabian for only a moment before turning her gaze to Damon. "And that Unholy Monster is still alive? What's the matter with you, Damon? If you won't do it, let me at him, and I'll show him and this *bastard child* of ours how to destroy a uniquely unholy vampire."

"Not so fast, Gabby. Before we destroy him, he informed me that he's arranged for all the vampires of the world to meet here before sunrise to attack us. There'll be thousands, if we can believe him."

"Oh, I think that's the first thing he's said that we can believe. It's got to be more than wishful thinking since he has no other vampires here to help him. Threatening us with that without it being true makes no sense." She looked to the West into the retreating darkness. "So, we have a lot of company coming. Thanks for nothing, Fabian.

"You're welcome. I hope you *enjoy* the infestation of my family before you *die!*"

Gabby handed the baby over to Damon, who kissed the baby gently on her forehead. "Looks like you, Thank God!"

"Okay, Damon, so, how do we prepare for this *infestation*, as Fabian describes it?"

"I'm not sure. Fabian's right in that our forces will be overrun by that many vampires. We may be able to destroy some, but not all. They do have the disadvantage of arriving just before dawn. If we can keep them occupied until then, the sun will destroy them all. However, if they outlast our troops, they can enter Fabian's mountain hideaway, and shut themselves in to formulate a plan to get ready for our subsequent attack. I don't want to give them that much time. They may come with something we haven't thought of."

Fabian laughed. "It won't matter! You'll all be dead by then. Ha, ha, ha, ha."

"He's right. We've got to have a better plan, but what?"

The baby stirred, and then morphed into a six-inch bat in Damon's arms, and squealed as loud as she could.

Gabby eyes springing open as far as they could. "That's it. That's the answer." She turned to Damon. "Destroy Fabian, and I'll give you *our* answer."

CHAPTER 70

WORLD VAMPIRE ATTACK

Asked to destroy Fabian by Gabby, Damon smiled. "With pleasure!"

Fabian screamed at him, "You disgrace your heritage! You're the Great Grandson Of The Marvelous Count Dracula. I spit on you."

The spittle dripped down Damon's face. Damon didn't bother to wipe it off.

Fabian watched the spittle on its slow journey. He shook his head. "You disgrace his name, his heritage, even his very existence as a vampire. The zombie part of you has overtaken the vampire part, and corrupted it in the worst possible way." He shook his head. "Disgusting!" He spat on Damon again, the spittle landing on Damon's cheek, and following the same torturous path as the other.

Damon lowered his head, and said, "Thank you, very much. That's the nicest thing you've ever said to me. We've wondered for a long time when that zombie part of us would rear its head. I believe you saw a major example of that *corruption* when you beheaded my beloved Gabby, and the zombie somehow enabled

265

her to reattach her head and body. Amazing! I'm not so sure that's a disgrace to my ancient ancestor. Who knows, he may agree with you, but for now, I'm happy he's not around to see our *corruption*, as you put it. It saved my wife, and allowed me have an amazing daughter." He placed a bent forefinger under his chin. "I can't wait to see what remarkable powers of regeneration she'll demonstrate. Time will tell. " He glared at Fabian. "But, of course, you won't be around to see any of that, now, will you?"

Fabian snarled back at Damon. "What happens to me is immaterial. Even if you do manage to destroy all of the vampires on their way here, there will still be small pockets of my colleagues around the world. They're the ones who couldn't respond for whatever reason to my call for help. They'll spread worldwide. They'll enroll many new humans as vampires…"

Gabby interrupted, "You mean they're going to bite those innocent humans, infecting them with your filth, don't you?"

Fabian's gaze shot to Gabby. "Of course! It's our way of spreading the vampire *gift*. We are the future of this world, not you." He shook, trying to dislodge himself from Damon's grip again. He snarled at his failure. "I don't care how you reconnected your head, or even if you are immortal. None of that matters! Those few groups of vampires left hunting around the world will seek revenge on you for the way you dealt with my vampire colleagues and me."

266

Nolan ran up to Damon, followed by Beecher and the rest of the SWAT team. "We have a great report for you two! We've had no one killed, or even bitten. It's surprising, really, with all that we faced. What have you got there, Damon?"

"Oh, simply the last of this vampire breed. He warned me that he's called a vampire convention here to attack us."

Nolan hung his head. "No! Don't tell me that. We just eliminated all the vampires and zombies in this clan. Now, we have more to deal with?" He shook his head. "You've got to be kidding."

Fabian shook his head. "No kidding, Human. Say your prayers because you and all your followers are about to be killed, or converted to vampires. Then, you'll understand how we think."

Beecher said, "We'll never understand your thinking. I can't imagine killing another individual to drink their blood, and, at the same time, condemn them to a life of vampirism. I'd rather die."

Fabian shrugged, as best he could beneath Damon's grip. "Your choice! All those vampires coming here any minute now will be starved for blood after their long trip. They'll mow through your forces as if you are fresh grass and they are sharp mower blades…no problem."

Nolan snarled at Fabian again, but said nothing.

Beecher stepped forward. "Let me at him. Give me the pleasure of destroying him." Gabby held up a stopping hand. She walked by Fabian toward Nolan. As she handed Nolan her daughter, she said, "May I please have your stake, and would you please hold my daughter?"

Nolan stuttered, "Your dau…dau…daughter?"

Gabby then turned to face Fabian. "I made you a promise to destroy you. I now fulfill that promise."

"Before you do, I want to warn you Zompires. There are only three of you now. As I said a little while ago, what happens to me is immaterial, even if my fellow vampires fail to destroy you and all your troops."

Gabby scowled at Fabian. "Really?"

He smiled. "Yes! You see, in the near future, and I do mean *near,* you'll be destroyed by your own species. My scientists, who you'll never be able to find, or stop, are developing Zompires from vampire DNA. It would have been easier with Damon's DNA to copy, but my scientists assure me, they are about to find out Damon's secrets hidden in his DNA. Its inevitable."

"You think so? I don't. Damon and I are committed to protecting all humankind from the likes of you…and I now extend that to any Zompire fiends your scientists invent. You can be sure of that."

A wry smile filled his face. "The only thing I'm sure of is that you are doomed."

Gabby stepped toward him, and screamed at the top of her lungs. She thrust the stake through Fabian's heart.

Fabian mimicked her scream as he melted into dust.

CHAPTER 71

BABY'S PLAN

Damon dropped his hand to his side as soon as the vampire had dissolved. He smiled. "I'm glad my wife keeps her promises...I think."

Gabby smiled back at Damon, but said nothing. Avoiding Fabian's dust, she returned to Nolan. "Yes, my daughter."

Nolan handed her daughter back to Gabby, and then turned to Damon. "Is it true what Fabian said about an impending vampire invasion?"

"Unfortunately, I believe he was telling the truth, although, I wish he wasn't. We may have hundreds, or even thousands of vampires coming to attack us."

Nolan dropped his head again. "So, how do we fight *them* off? How do we prepare for them?" He shook his head. "We don't have the element of surprise working for us. We can destroy a few of them with stakes as they come at us, but, with those numbers, we can't sustain the upper hand very long before they overwhelm us. We can't win."

Beecher came to Nolan's side. "But we can try. We don't have any choice. We've got to try.

Otherwise, the whole world will be at their disposal. I don't like the thought of the remaining Humans serving as the blood-food for these fiends, especially if I had the chance to stop them, and failed."

Damon turned to Gabby. "Any ideas?"

"Not really. You?"

He shook his head. "I was hoping you'd come to our rescue with a boatload of ideas."

"No such luck. Even if we turn into gigantic bats, or Eagles, there's no way we can destroy that many vampire bats. Suppose they're as large as us." She gazed upon the police gathering around her. "There's no way these human policemen, despite their expertise with stakes, can possibly hold off the vampire horde either. They would be a great help undoubtedly, but to win, we'll have to destroy every one of them." She shook her head. "Impossible!"

The baby in her arms suddenly shook, and converted into a small bat in Gabby's hand.

Gabby opened her eyes wide. "What is it, Honey?"

The bat grew to a one-foot long bat, turned its head skyward, and squealed its radar-seeking voice.

Gabby again asked, "What is it, Oh Daughter of Mine…and Daddy Damon's, of course?"

The shrill scream again filled the mountainside.

Both Gabby and Damon looked skyward and at the mountainside, a sheer cliff of granite. Damon gazed at Gabby, and shrugged his shoulders.

Gabby smiled. "I wonder…"

"Again with the *wonder*? You wonder what?"

Our very smart daughter is giving us an example of her idea."

"Which is what? I don't get it."

"Well, the noise she's making is the one that finds our way as bats, using radar. Right?"

"Sure, all bats use it to *see* things in front of them."

"Right! So, our adversaries should be here before light. They'll be in a rush to either find us to attack, or to find shelter inside that mountain. In the relative darkness, they'll still need their radar to find us, and to attack us."

"So?"

"So, if their radar is disrupted, or interfered with, they won't be able to find us."

"That won't help us much. Sure, we can kill a few of them, but even with limited *vision*, we can't eliminate all of them. If they reach the inside of the mountain, and lock the gate, we won't be able to get in. They would then come out at night to fight us. That gives them the big advantage again." He turned his attention to his daughter. "Well, Daughter, what have you got in mind? How is disrupting their radar any help to us?"

The bat screeched again.

Gabby shot her finger into the air, and screamed, "Of course! I've got it, now. Smart girl! The three of us can do it together."

Her baby squealed again, this time toward the West, as a swarm of bats could be seen headed their way.

CHAPTER 72

VAMPIRE BAT SWARM

Damon turned to Gabby. "Explain, please, and quick before the hordes get here."

Gabby nodded, as she turned her attention to her daughter. "Okay, Little One, listen! First, you enlarge to the largest bat you can." Gabby turned to Damon as the small bat enlarged to ten feet tall with a wing span over twenty feet, and turned to the West.

Gabby smiled, and shook her head. "You know, we *really* have to take the time to name our daughter. She deserves it."

"Fine, but can we take care of the vampires first?" Damon brought the palms of his hands together, as if praying. "Please?"

"Okay. Those incoming vampire bats got here using their radar in place of light vision. Right?"

"Of course. We've already established that. So what?"

"If we jam that radar with our own radar, that should prevent them from *seeing* us, or, more importantly, seeing that huge mountain cliff behind us."

Damon nodded. "Oh, I get it now. Disrupt their flight pattern so they can't see us, or the safety of the darkness within Fabian's cave. Head them toward the mountain cliff."

"Exactly! I'm hoping we can direct them right into the mountain. That will give us the opportunity to destroy them."

Damon frowned. "But with so many of them coming, even if we knocked them out, or at least stunned them, it would take hours to pierce their hearts with those spears. Have to think of a quicker way."

Beecher ran up to Damon. "I may have a solution for that. I brought along a flamethrower. If I use that as they hit the ground, will that suffice?"

Gabby smiled. "Oh, I think that would work nicely. Don't use it until they're all down, though. I'm not sure what would happen if you threw flames into their flight pattern. Some may divert to the side, and avoid not only the flames, but the entire mountain as well. Better to get all of them to the ground first."

Beecher ran into the surrounding woods to retrieve the flamethrower. As he ran, he yelled over his shoulder. "Not to worry. I've been itching to use this thing ever since we got here. Don't worry! I'll follow your directions."

Nolan covered his face with one hand. "Oh, God, you may have released the *Beecher apocalypse* on us."

Damon laughed. "As long as he aims that thing at those vampires, and it becomes *their* apocalypse, not ours, we're okay with that."

Gabby turned her head sideways. "I hear their wings flapping, and I can detect their radar beeps. They're close. Quick, Damon, change into the largest bat you can. Let's get ready to screech as loud as the three of us can to disrupt their radar."

Nolan said. "This better work."

A second before converting to a bat, Gabby said, "It will. My so-far unnamed daughter is brilliant! If she thinks it will work, it will. Nolan, hide your troops, in case this doesn't work the way we think it should. Your men shouldn't hear our high-pitched screeches, but, in case some of them do, have all of them cover their ears. Damon and Beautiful Unnamed Daughter, wait for my screech to start yours, and make it loud!"

Damon smiled. "She must take after her mother. She understands our speech without us ever teaching her, and she comes up with brilliant ideas, like when you agreed to marry me." He smiled. "I promise, Gabby, we'll name her as soon as this is over." With that, he converted to a bat that grew larger and larger until he was over 20 feet in length. He joined his wife and daughter at over forty feet in the air, hovering there. All three faced West.

A loud flapping sound scorched the air, soon followed by a black cloud of vampire bats. As they were one hundred yards from the clearing in front of the mountain, Gabby opened her beak, and screeched as loud as she could, mimicking the sound emanating from the bats. Her family joined her in the effort. The deafening, flapping sound of the vampire horde soared closer.

CHAPTER 73

VAMPIRE DESTRUCTION

As the vampire horde approached the Zompires, the three Zompires dropped to the ground, giving them direct access to the mountainside. The Zompire trio continued their disruptive screeching even as the vampire bats began colliding with the mountain, and fell to the ground. As the first few crashed, and fell toward the ground, some of the following bats detected their falling, and dove toward the ground to avoid an 'unseen' obstacle that they had not detected. This surprised Gabby, who thought their screeching would disrupt all of the vampire bats' direction-finding radar.

Luckily, the large majority of the vampire bats did not have such a sensitive radar system, and continued on what they thought was a clear passage, crashing headlong into the mountainside.

Gabby converted to her human form, and ran toward the bats that had avoided their mountainside welcome. As she ran, she yelled over her shoulder, "Stay in bat form, and continue to broadcast. I'll take care of those that avoided our trap." She ran at top Zompire speed, picking up the small bats, the largest around 6 inches in length, that had avoided the mountain trap, and instead had landed on the ground to get their new bearing. With all her might, she threw these bats against the mountainside, where they landed, helpless and unconscious, with their comrades.

Seeing a couple of vampire bats that had transformed into their vampire-human form, she ran toward them. Along the way, she picked up two unconscious vampire bats, one in each hand, and thrust them with all her Zompire might into the temples of the vampire-humans. The beaks of the bats penetrated deep into their brains. They collapsed at her feet. She picked up both bodies by their collars, and tossed them onto the pile of vampire bats.

Nolan and Beecher had emerged from their forest-hiding place, and now ran toward her as the last of the vampire bats topped the vampire pile. Beecher wore a flamethrower backpack, and carried the flamethrower nozzle using both hands.

Gabby nodded, adding as she passed the policemen, "Burn them! Burn them *all* real good, Beecher."

Beecher smiled, and stopped his advance at the edge of the now three-foot deep vampire pile. He ignited the flamethrower, and sprayed its flame over the pile. The bats ignited quickly. The flames grew to the level of the top of the mountain. The other policemen retreated from the heat of the fire.

Nolan stood beside Beecher. "Make sure you burn them to a crisp. I don't want any of them coming back as…who knows what?"

"Got it! Don't worry! I plan to empty the entire fuel canister onto them. I'll make sure there's only cinders left."

Nolan nodded. "Good, but sift through those cinders anyway. Crush, or burn further, anything bigger than a walnut. I don't want any of those cinders reforming as vampires. I'll feel safer that way."

"One toasted walnut coming up. Right! Burnt to a crisp and crushed! Don't worry! I've been looking forward to using this thing against these fiends for a long time. Besides, I'm enjoying this."

Nolan turned to walk toward the Zompires, now converted to their human-Zompire form. Damon held the human baby close. "I'm afraid you're enjoying it a little too much, Beecher. Save some fuel, though, in case a few vampire bats are latecomers. We may need to fry them too."

"Will do!"

CHAPTER 74

BABY'S NAME

Gabby smiled as Nolan approached her. "Good job, Nolan."

Nolan turned toward the huge blaze. "Thanks. You'd better save some of that *thanks* for Beecher. He's having a ball burning them to a crisp."

"Glad he's having such a good time. More importantly, those vampire bats are gone forever, especially if Beecher follows your instructions, and disrupts the cinders."

Nolan nodded. "Yeah, I think it's better to be safe than sorry, as they say. I don't know if they can return after being incinerated, but why take the chance?"

Damon shielded his eyes from the blaze. "I believe there is a way to return the vampire to existence once they are destroyed into dust, or even burned. It is rumored that human, or, even better, vampire blood dripped onto the dust or cinders will bring them back. That is something I don't want to experiment with right now, however. So, make sure those cinders are buried well, and don't let anyone near the ashes if they've got a cut that may drip onto the vampires. Having Beecher disrupt the ashes should help also."

Nolan nodded. "Will do."

Damon then handed the Zompire-human baby to her mother. "I think this belongs to you."

"I believe she belongs to both of us. Have you thought of any names for our brilliant Zompire-child?"

Damon shook his head. "No, but I think she should be named by you. She obviously takes after her mother in intelligence and forethought planning. After all, she did come up with the plan to destroy all those vampire bats descending upon us. By the way, how did she do all that? I mean, she understood all of our speech, and figured out how to disrupt the vampires' radar to give us the advantage. How is that possible?"

"I don't know for sure, but that tells me she has a great future in vampire hunting. She can help us hunt down, and destroy any vampires who didn't make this...*reunion*...of sorts."

"Agreed! Now, what are you going to name her? How about *Vampire-Huntress*?"

"No, that's too obvious, and once they're all destroyed, it's a useless moniker." Gabby placed a crooked finger under her chin, thinking deeply. Her gaze fell to the baby in her arms. "I've got it! If, as you said, she's brilliant like her mother, she should carry that name...or at least a part of it. How about

Riella? It's a shortened form of my given name, *Gabriella*. She can call herself anything she wants once she's grown, 'Ria,' or 'Ella,' 'Riella,' or anything she wants."

Damon laughed. "She'll probably be as strong willed as her mother, and she'll pick her own name. *Riella* sounds great to me to for now." He caressed the baby's chin with his hand. "What do you think, *Riella*?"

Riella's eyes widened, she chuckled, burped and nodded.

Damon smiled. "*Riella* it is then. He looked Heavenward, and fist pumped upward as he yelled, "The three Zompires are here to protect Humanity from the Vampire virus. There's no way any of them will survive our search and destroy mission."

Gabby held Riella above her head to her arms' length. "Amen to that! Amen to that!"

Riella screeched.

All three Zompires laughed.

<u>END</u>

Zephaniah 1:1-7, 14-2:3

...And their blood shall be poured out like dust,
And their brains like dung...

Made in the USA
Middletown, DE
11 September 2021